BODY PART

CW00521479

SERIES THREE BOOK THREE

John Gammon achieves a dream in this tense thriller set in the Peak District.

Ride this rollercoaster of emotion with Detective John Gammon. Experience the highs and lows that follow in our hero's life.

With a monster loose in the beautiful Peak District of Derbyshire it's going to take every ounce of his being to solve this case if he can.

Series Three
Book Three
in the John Gammon Detective Series

This is my first book where a promotion has been used for a place as a Detective Inspector at Bixton Police Station. The winner is **Mr *Daniel Kiernan*** now immortalised in this book as Detective Inspector Danny Kiernan.

During the competition I was contacted by a friend of the singing duo Brian and Michael. Michelle Miles is a friend of the duo. They had a number one hit with a song based on LS Lowry called 'Matchstalk Men and Matchstalk Cats and Dogs'. She nominated one of them. She didn't win but thank you for entering. So the competition proved to be a massive success. The names were collated, and the winner picked out. Thanks to everybody who took the time to take part and I hope Mr Kiernan likes his character.

BODY PARTS

My thanks to Kevin and Doreen, two of the main characters in all the books, for their support in my writing career. I hope they have enjoyed being part of this journey.

My best wishes for their retirement.

Series Three
Book Three
in the John Gammon Detective Series

This book is a work of fiction. Names, characters, organisations, places, events and incidents are either products of the author's imagination or are used fictitiously.
All rights reserved.

BODY PARTS

Enjoy this thrilling detective series set in the beautiful Peak District.

Colin J Galtrey has nineteen books now available, thirteen are John Gammon detective books. There is also a Trilogy to read and three stand-alone books all in different genres.

Please take the time to browse my website which also gives you a short history of our beautiful Peak District.

www.colingaltrey.co.uk

**Series Three
Book Three
in the John Gammon Detective Series**

Contents

BODY PARTS

CHAPTER ONE

Months had passed and with all cases closed life seemed quite slow for DI Gammon, that was until the phone rang in his office.

"Yes, Sergeant?"

"A young man has been found dead in Dilley Dale, Sir. I have asked DI Lee and DI Smarty to attend and I have also sent forensics."

"Good man, I will make my way there now."

Gammon set off for Dilley Dale. From a distance he could see the blue lights flashing and the main village road cordoned off. Gammon showed his warrant card to the PC guarding entry.

"Good morning, Sir," said the young PC.

"Yes, good morning, Constable."

Lee was talking to a woman and Smarty was talking to an elderly gentleman. Gammon made his way to the obligatory white tent where Wally's team was. He put his head inside which always sent Wally apoplectic, and he would then come out of the tent lecturing Gammon on scene contamination.

"Good morning Wally. What we got?"

"A male, I would say between twenty five and thirty with a severed arm."

"Anything else?"

"Not that I have found yet, but I think he bled to death."

"Ok, can I have a name and something to work on for 9.00 am, Wally?"

"You are a task master John. I will do my best."

BODY PARTS

Gammon rang back to desk Sergeant Beeney to arrange a meeting in the incident room.

"Is DCI Dirk in yet?"

"He is away on a course for two weeks Sir."

"Oh yeah, forgot about that Warren. I will be back in a bit."

Gammon wandered over to DI Lee who had just finished with the woman.

"What we got, Peter?"

"Nothing really John, she was at the scene when the body was found."

"Does she know the man?"

"She said she remembered him from the toy factory, but she didn't know him, and she left not long after he started."

"When did the toy factory close?"

"It's got to be getting on for seven years now. They demolished it when all the work went to China, and that's where those new houses are now."

"Nothing else though Peter?"

"No, that's it John."

"Have you taken her name and address?"

Lee looked at his notebook.

"Her name is Stella Watkins. She lives at number fourteen, Stinton Close."

"What you got, Dave?"

"The guy that found the body, a Mr John Glew, was out running. He is training for the Ackbourne Half Marathon and found the body dumped at the side of the road. He said it he thought it was a badger from a distance because there are so many of them dead at the side of the road these days. Mr Glew rang Bixton Police, hence all this lot."

"Ok, you got his address etc. Dave?"

"Yes John."

BODY PARTS

"Ok lads, not a lot we can do here. I'll let one of you two buy the bacon sandwiches at Beryl's Butties."

"Sounds good to me, John."

They arrived at Beryl's Butties and ordered three coffees and three doorstep bacon butties.

"Never been here before, John."

"Best breakfast anywhere, Dave."

"I agree, John."

"I used to come here a lot when I was a young Sergeant. Misspent youth."

Peter and John laughed.

They had almost finished their sandwiches when John got a call. He didn't recognise the number so assumed it must be PPI. He excused himself and went to his car and called the number back.

"John, it's Anouska. I said I would let you know you have a little girl, eight pounds one ounce. I am going to call her Anka after my grandma and Emily after your mother you spoke about, so she will be Anka Emily."

John was silent. He didn't know if he should laugh or cry. A baby girl. They hadn't had the DNA test done yet and it wasn't the right time.

"Anouska, text me your bank details and I will set up a direct debit with my bank."

"There is time for that John. I have to go now my parents are here. She is beautiful John, I will send you a photograph," and she hung up.

John didn't know what to do, but he knew one person he could trust, and that was Kev at The Spinning Jenny. He thought he would call in on his way home that night.

There was a tap on the car window.

"You ok mate?"

"Oh yeah, sorry Dave, bloody PPI again. I will see you back at the station."

On the way back all John could think about was Anouska and the baby. He finally arrived at Bixton and the first person he met on the stairs was DI Scooper. Sandra was a friend and had been a lover many times. He just wished he could share the news, but it wasn't appropriate with Sandra losing their baby some time back.

"Hi John, sad thing about that young man, DI Lee was just telling me."

"Yeah, dreadful Sandra. We have a meeting in the incident room at 9.00am."

"Yes, Sergeant Beeney told all of us, John."

"Meant to say I've got a spare ticket for Bixton Opera House on Saturday. Billy Whizz the comedian is on for one night only. I was going with an old school friend, but she can't make it Saturday so do you want to come?"

"Can do, that would be nice. Why don't we have a meal at that Italian?"

"Oh yeah, Luigi Duce."

"That's the one."

"Ok John, I will book it for 6.00pm. Do you want me to drive?"

"No, I'll pick you up at 5.15pm."

"Great, look forward to it."

"Best crack on Sandra, need to tell Dirk about this murder."

"Good luck with that one, John."

Gammon grabbed a cup of coffee and did his paperwork until 5.00pm. He was desperate to talk to Kev so left on time to head for the Spinning Jenny.

John entered the pub where Jane Halzimmer was working, Kev was engrossed at the end of the bar with his Sporting Life.

"Hello John, how are you?"

"Good, thanks Jane. I saw Gary Lewis the other morning. Does he work for Phil Sterndale a bit?"

"Not my boyfriend anymore, John."

"There you go again Mr Gammon putting your foot in it," and Kev laughed.

"Get John a Pedigree please Jane, and a bottle of Low C for me."

"Want you a minute mate, can I have a quiet word?"

"Yeah, grab a seat mate, I will bring the beer over."

Series Three
Book Three
in the John Gammon Detective Series

John got by the fire feeling lucky that Carol Lestar wasn't in, or she would have gone mental. She likes to think that's her seat he thought. Kev came over with a pint for John and a bottle of Low C for himself.

"Now then lad, what's troubling you?"

"Look mate, you are the only one I can tell other than Steve. But after what he's been through it would be a bit insensitive of me to tell him."

"I'm a dad."

"What?"

"Remember Anouska? She left because she was pregnant by me."

Kev looked bemused.

"Are you sure, lad?"

"Yes, positive Kev. It's a little girl, Anka Emily."

"Is she coming back?"

"No, I will support her though."

BODY PARTS

"Look John, you are a clever guy, are you sure it's yours?"

"I know it is, Kev."

"Then I won't say anymore, other than congratulations."

"Please keep this to yourself Kev. I don't want it getting out for obvious reasons."

"Understand lad, you know me, if you tell me something that's a secret it will never leave my lips, I promise. Right we best wet the baby's head. Bring me a bottle of Napoleon brandy, please Jane."

"What are we celebrating, Kevin?"

"Nothing really, just we haven't had a brandy session in ages. Doreen is having her hair done, so will be out for ages and she won't be bothered, because she will be having a session with her mate the hairdresser."

Series Three
Book Three
in the John Gammon Detective Series

John and Kev had half the bottle by the time Doreen and the hairdresser, Michelle, came in and joined them.

"Like the new short haircut, Doreen."

"Yes, I'm pleased with it, aren't I Michelle?"

"You said you were."

John poured them both a brandy and topped his and Kev's glasses up.

"So, how's the handsome detective then?"

John laughed pretending to look around for him.

"I hear you are single again."

"Who told you that?"

"Sandra Scooper's mum. She has her hair done at my salon. She said you had a soft spot for her daughter."

John could feel his colour rising. Doreen bailed him out.

BODY PARTS

"It's most probably the other way around Michelle, he even cost us our barmaid."

Kev nearly chocked on his brandy.

"I'm only joking. She went home, but she wanted to get her claws into John, didn't she, love?" and playfully tweaked his cheek. John was now bright red with embarrassment.

It was almost 11.30pm when he decided to call it a night and headed to the cottage.

John opened the kitchen door and on the Matt was a letter. On the address it just said 'Cure'.

The writing was very precise. It read.
'Dear Mr Gammon,

I realise the people you have arrested for the murders using sodium hypochlorite were guilty of the crimes, but you need to understand it's for the greater good, Mr Gammon.

Series Three
Book Three
in the John Gammon Detective Series

Because of people like that, medicine is where it is today. Sadly, Miss Darnell is the latest victim and that is down to me. I really thought I had mastered the doses and Miss Darnell did so well. I am sorry for her family but like I said, it is for the greater good.

You will find Miss Darnell in the bushes by the old railwayman's crossing at Dilley Dale. I tried to make her last hour as dignified as possible.

If you don't understand now, one day I hope you will. We don't want to kill people but there are bound to be casualties on the way.'

The letter wasn't signed.

John phoned Di Trimble at the station and told her to get Wally and the team to Dilley Dale Donkey Crossing, as he affectionately knew it. He also said to get

BODY PARTS

DI Milton and DI Scooper down there, and to ask DI Scooper to pick him up from his cottage.

Sandra arrived. It was now 12.40am just what he needed after a night on the brandy with Kev.

"Blimey, I can smell alcohol on you John, have you been drinking at home?"

"No, just got back from the Spinning Jenny. I had a bit of a session with Kev."

"Don't you ever learn?"

John told Sandra about the letter. He wanted her thoughts on it.

"The letter sounds a bit medical, but is it meant to, so that it throws us off the scent of the real killer?"

"Yes, you could be right. It's very well written and quite articulate. That's all we need Sandra. It's clearly a throwback to the cult days, so how many of these nutters are out there?"

"Guess we may find out in the coming months," Sandra replied as they arrived at Donkey Crossing.

"Thought this was put to bed, John."

"So did I, Carl. It looks like we don't know how many of these people there are out there with these beliefs."

John handed Wally the envelope in a clear plastic bag.

"Bloody hell John, you are making my team have it. Depending on what time we get done here, can we make the morning meeting about the guy with the severed left arm at 10.00am instead of 9.00am?"

"Ok it's a deal Wally, as long as you can tell me about this guy as well."

"You don't bloody want much John, do you?"

BODY PARTS

Gammon laughed and walked back to the car, telling DI Smarty that he was going to get the address of the poor girl and see the parents to break the news.

Gammon rang the station to get an address of Miss Darnell. Di Trimble came back with a Sally Darnell, Pond Cottage, Pommie. Gammon decided it was too risky and he would wait for Wally in the morning. He didn't want to get somebody up in the middle of the night and it turn out not to be their daughter.

Gammon got Scooper to run him back home and he tried to get a few hours sleep before getting back to the cases in question at the station.

John woke at 6.00am with a mouth like the bottom of a budgie cage. Why do I do this to myself he thought?

Series Three
Book Three
in the John Gammon Detective Series

He was in work for 7.30am and thought he would get some paperwork done, before the meeting at 10.00am with Wally and the team. He instructed Sergeant Beeney to tell everyone as they arrived at the meeting was now 10.00am.

The hours passed quite quickly, and Gammon made his way downstairs to the incident room.

"Ok everyone, some night eh? Right we have two dead bodies on our hands. Wally what do you know?"

"Ok, the man with the severed arm is Alan Hewitt. We have checked dental records and DNA. He was on our database. He had an altercation about three weeks back with a guy outside Sandie's Disco in Micklock, so we know one hundred percent he is the man. DS Magic found the address."

BODY PARTS

Magic stood up. "He lives with a Gemma Adley, at 117 Beau Vista, Micklock."

"Ok, anything else Wally?"

"Yes, Mr Hewitt died from the loss of his arm. He appeared to have been drugged then dumped at the Donkey Crossing at Dilley Dale."

"So, was he murdered there?"

"I believe he was murdered somewhere else then dumped. Mr Hewitt had steroids in his system, which looking at his body I would say he was a body builder."

"Anything else, Wally?"

"Yes, whoever cut off his left arm knew how to dismember a body."

"What are we saying, the killer was possibly a surgeon?"

"Either that or a bloody good butcher."

This made the detectives laugh.

Series Three
Book Three
in the John Gammon Detective Series

"Ok calm down. Right Wally, moving on to the supposed Miss Darnell."

"This is a whole different story. The sodium, sorry for you numpties bleach, had been administered over possibly eight or ten weeks in very small doses. I would say on a daily basis."

Smarty put his hand up.

"What are we saying here? We have another serial killer and if so, is this as we first thought, some kind of cult?"

Gammon stood up.

"In reply to your question Dave, I do believe it's a cult of some kind."

"How many of them are out there?"

"I really don't know. I think, we all thought this was over from previously but clearly not. So we go again, as they say it doesn't rain but it pours."

BODY PARTS

"Wally did you get anything from the letter?"

"Nothing, John."

"Ok, pass it over. I will read it out so we all know what we are playing with."

Wally handed Gammon the letter.

"Dear Mr Gammon

I realise the people you have arrested for the murders using sodium hypochlorite were guilty of the crimes, but you need to understand it's for the greater good, Mr Gammon.

Because of people like that medicine is where it is today. Sadly, Miss Darnell is the latest victim and that is down to me. I really thought I had mastered the doses and Miss Darnell did so well. I am sorry for her family but like I said, it is for the greater good.

Series Three
Book Three
in the John Gammon Detective Series

You will find Miss Darnell in the bushes by the old railway man's crossing at Dilley Dale. I tried to make her last hour as dignified as possible.

If you don't understand now, one day I hope you will we don't want to kill people but there are bound to be casualties on the way."

"As you would expect the letter wasn't signed."

Scooper put her hand up.

"That's a medical guy in my opinion."

This created a reaction, both Milton and Lee disagreed. They both thought it was a copycat killing nothing do with any sect.

"Well whichever way we look at it whoever carried out the latest killing needs finding and quick."

BODY PARTS

"Sandra and Carl, visit Mark Block. If your hunch is right let's see if we can get a reaction."

"Dave and Peter, I want the severed arm victim's bank accounts looking at find where he worked etc."

"Myself and DS Yap will go and tell the bad news to both the victim's next of kin."

"Magic, I want you to look at the initial suspects in these bleach murders. Who is left that we might think could still be involved?"

With that Gammon ended the meeting.

"Come on DS Yap, not the nicest bit of the job."

Gammon and Yap set off for 117 Beau Vista, Micklock, the home Alan Hewitt which he shared with Gemma Hadley. Gammon knocked on the small oak door of 117 Beau Vista in Micklock. The row of houses had reputedly been work houses many years ago but were done up in the late nineties and looked quite stunning.

Gammon rang the bell three times. A voice from inside shouted, "Wait a minute, I haven't got skates on"

Eventually the door opened and young lady in her mid-twenties answered the door. Gammon and Yap showed her their warrant cards.

"Go on then, now what has he been up to? I knew he should have come skiing with me."

"May we step inside, Miss Hadley?"

"Yes of course, this sound serious. My bloody bloke and his temper."

"Please take a seat Miss Hadley."

Gemma Hadley sat down.

"Whatever is a matter?"

BODY PARTS

"I am very sorry to say, but Mr Hewitt has been found murdered."

"What is this, some kind of wind up?"

"I wish it was, Miss Hadley."

Gemma just sat in amazement, then the tears flowed. The poor girl had just come back from a skiing holiday so would not have known he was even missing.

"This isn't pleasant, but Mr Hewitt's left arm was severed, and not at the crime scene. Do you know of anybody that he knew who would be capable of doing this?"

"He was a bouncer, Mr Gammon. He made enemies, that's the nature of the job."

"Where was he a door-man?"

"Sandie's in Micklock."

"Which gym did he attend? Without doubt he worked out and steroids were found in his system."

Series Three
Book Three
in the John Gammon Detective Series

"I told him to stop taking them Mr Gammon, but he was addicted to having this pumped up body. He went seven days a week to Muscles Gym in Cramford."

"Ok well, I will let you grieve in peace. Has he any family that could identify the body and do you need somebody to sit with you?"

"No, Mr Gammon. I will call my sister, she was coming over anyway. No, Alan adopted when he was two years old. His adopted parents were killed on a level crossing in Micklock."

"What about his biological parents, did he know who they were?"

"He said he didn't want to know, but I researched it and found that his mother had been a crack addict in Liverpool and had died. His father was in the army and was killed in Iraq, so I let sleeping dogs lie."

BODY PARTS

"Ok, could you come to Bixton in the morning and formally identify Mr Hewitt?

"Yes, I will. What time?"

"Well if I say 11.00am, would that be ok?"

"Yes, that's fine."

"Look here is my card, if you need anything just call night or day."

"Very kind of you Mr Gammon, but I will be ok."

Gammon and Yap left Gemma Hadley wiping tears from her face as they left the driveway and headed for Pommie and Sally Darnell's parents.

"See what you mean Sir, not a nice part of the job. You must have done a few."

"Yes, I have Ian, but it doesn't become any easier."

They drove through the winding roads of Pommie, past the church then took a sharp left to the bottom of the dale, and Pond Cottage home of Sally Darnell's parents.

The little cottage had wisteria growing over the door and was absolutely stunning. An elderly gentleman was pruning some roses in the immaculately cared for garden.

"Can I help you?" he said in quiet but correctly spoken manner.

"Are you Mr Darnell?"

"Yes, how can I help you?"

Just then a lady in her early fifties came to the door.

"Who is it, dad?" she said.

Gammon quickly realised that this was possibly Sally Darnell's grandfather. Both Gammon and Yap showed their warrant cards.

"How can I help you?"

"Are you Mrs Darnell, mother of Sally Darnell?"

BODY PARTS

"Yes."

"Told you she would do something stupid, Christine."

"Be quiet, dad."

"May we come into the house, Mrs Darnell."

Christine Darnell showed them into the living room, which was very neat with a nice three-piece suite and flowery curtains.

"Please take a seat," she said. "Would you like a drink?"

"Thank you, Mrs Darnell, but we are fine."

"So, what has our Sally done?"

"Please take a seat Mrs Darnell. I am afraid we have bad news for you. Your daughter Sally was found last night at Dilley Dale. She had been murdered."

"No, you have that wrong. About eight weeks ago we argued, she had been staying out a lot, not coming home, not telling us where she was. She had met this bloke at work."

"Do you have a name for this bloke?"

She only said his name was Kevin, but she said we were nosey. Anyway, two days after the argument she didn't come home, and she told us she was going travelling with her boyfriend. That was the last we have heard from her."

"This Kevin guy, did she meet him socially or at work?"

"Pretty sure it was somebody she worked with at the hospital in Micklock. Sally was the manager of the restaurant, you know the ones in hospitals that sell what my husband calls pub food. My husband Seth hated that we had put her through university, and she achieved a Masters Degree in psychology, then never used it.

BODY PARTS

Sally could be a bit of a rebel, Mr Gammon."

By now the old guy had come in.

"Rebel? I told you when she was sixteen she needed her arse tanning, she was a bad apple that one."

"Oh, be quiet dad, the world's a different place from when you were a teenager."

The old guy shuffled off to the kitchen muttering.

"So, you see Mr Gammon, our Sally is away."

"I know you possibly don't believe this, or even want to believe it, but I do need you to identify the body, please Mrs Darnell."

"I don't see why, but I will if it helps you."

Series Three
Book Three
in the John Gammon Detective Series

"Could you come to Bixton at 3.00pm and ask for a John Walvin. He will conduct the situation."

"Ok Mr Gammon, but I hope you find the poor girl's parents."

Gammon and Yap left.

"Do you think we have the wrong person, Sir?"

"No, I don't Ian. Our next port of call is the hospital, and let's see if there is a Kevin to speak to."

Gammon and Yap arrived at Micklock hospital which was quite modern and very big.

"I don't know how older people get around this place, Sir."

"Never mind older, I think I would struggle it's so big."

"Let's head for the cafeteria or restaurant as Mrs Darnell calls it."

BODY PARTS

It was now almost 3.00pm and most visitors that called for lunch or a coffee had gone. It was perfect to question the two girls behind the counter. Gammon ordered two coffees and two lemon drizzle cakes. Then he showed one of the girls his warrant card.

"Could we have a word please?"

The young looked a little fazed by this but followed them to a seat that Ian had found.

The young girl sat down.

"You are?"

"Oh, ugh, Tammie Wyatt."

"Ok Tammie, it's only a few questions. I believe you work with Sally Darnell?"

"Well I did do, but she packed the job in about eight week ago to go travelling with her boyfriend."

"Who was her boyfriend?"

"She said his name was Kevin."

"Did you meet him?"

"No, we wondered if it was made up. One of the junior doctor was always chatting her up and we thought it was just cover. She didn't want people to know she was seeing a junior doctor, but then she left to go travelling with this Kevin. The junior doctor still comes every day for a coffee so we must have got it wrong."

"Do you know the name of the junior doctor?"

"I'm not sure, but my friend does. She fancied the pants off him."

"Marilyn, who is that junior doctor you like? You know, the good looking one that was always chatting to Sally before she left."

"Oh, you mean Mark?"

"Mark who?"

BODY PARTS

"Mark Block. He is bloody gorgeous. Why all these questions, Mr Gammon?"

"Oh nothing. I think I am barking up the wrong tree, but thank you for your time."

The girls left Gammon and Yap. Yap had almost finished his cake because Gammon had done all the talking.

"Come on Ian, back to the station."

"Bloody hell Sir, is it that Mark Block from Beerly Moor?"

"Not sure yet Ian, but I am going to get a search warrant for tomorrow. I don't want him getting suspicious."

"Do you think he did both murders, Darnell and Hewitt, with them both being at Dilley Dale?"

"No, I think that is a coincidence Ian."

They arrived back at Bixton Police Station and Gammon went straight to

Wally to check that Mrs Darnell had confirmed that was indeed her daughter. Wally said she had, and she was obviously upset so they had called her husband.

"Very sad, Wally."

"We see too many, John."

Gammon left Wally and returned to his office.

He decided the next day to ask Micklock Hospital for all records of doctors and junior doctors with the name of Kevin.

The time now was 6.10pm so Gammon left deciding to get a carry-out meal from the Spinning Jenny.

"Goodnight Sergeant."

"Yes, goodnight Sir."

John took the scenic route to Swinster. It was a beautiful night, made all the more enjoyable when his phone signalled he had

BODY PARTS

a WhatsApp message and picture from Anouska. His little girl Anka, with her mother Anouska. It quite made John's day. He just wished he could share his happiness.

John clicked off his phone and made his way down the well-worn stone steps into the quaint bar area of the Spinning Jenny. Joni was behind the bar, there was no sign of Kev though.

"Where's the main man, Joni?"

"Who, Kev?"

"Yeah."

"He has been out all day. They have gone to the races in York and are stopping up there. Why?"

"Oh, I fancied a carry-out, but it doesn't matter."

Series Three
Book Three
in the John Gammon Detective Series

"Time you settled down John, with a good woman," Joni said in a slightly sarcastic tone.

John didn't rise to it and ordered a pint.

"What's that, Joni?"

"Oh, Kev has got Pants on Yer Head Bob to do a comedy act, and there is a local group playing called The Calculators. They play sixties and seventies music."

"When is it on? I can't see from here."

"This Saturday John, there's no charge. Are you coming?"

"Well I guess so, what about you?"

"Doreen asked me to work with Jane Halzimmer and Kev behind the bar."

"Shame that, we could have had a dance."

"You never change Mr Gammon. do you?" and she laughed.

BODY PARTS

The pub didn't fill up much, so John left at 10.00pm and headed home. Once inside he made a strong coffee and took it upstairs. He decided he wanted to try and finish a book he had started called SCARAB FALLS. John had quite enjoyed the book set in the seventies at the height of the Irish troubles. At almost midnight, with still a good third of the book to go, John nodded off.

The following morning on the way in DI Smarty rang to say the warrant had come through to search Mark Block's house again. This was perfect, because if Block was involved he wouldn't have had much time to sort or cover his tracks. Gammon said he would meet the team at Poppy's Farm on Beerly Moor. If he arrived after them, they were to wait before approaching the farm. He had rung Sergeant Magic and asked him to find out from Micklock Hospital Administration department if they had a Kevin that was a doctor or Junior doctor at Micklock.

Gammon arrived just as the rest of the team were arriving. Smarty handed John the search warrant for Poppy Mill, the home of Mark Block.

Gammon knocked on the old door and Block came to the door.

"Good morning Mr Gammon, how can I help you?"

"Mr Block, I have a warrant here to search these premises including any outbuildings on this site."

Block looked shaken.

"I will then ask you to accompany me to Bixton Police station for further questioning."

BODY PARTS

"Ok team, in you go."

They brushed past Block with Scooper, Lee and Yap going upstairs, and Gammon. Smarty and Milton taking downstairs. Block was watching. A good thirty minutes passed with nothing to show for their efforts.

"Ok, let's take a look outside."

Block let them get on with it which Gammon thought was odd. It was like he was saying you won't find anything. Gammon instructed Sergeant Magic to stay with Block.

The first two buildings they found nothing. In the third building Smarty noticed a trap door which had been partially covered with straw to disguise it. He pulled up the door and there was a set of wooden steps with lights. On the wall were pictures of the original cult, then a picture of the others. Across the top in chalk somebody had written '*One day they will thank us*'. Gammon opened a red day diary. Inside were the doses that poor Sally Darnell had been given, with the final comment saying 'Dead'.

"Get up there Smarty and arrest him for the murder of Sally Darnell. Sandra get Wally over here to see what he can find."

Smarty ran across to the house. Sergeant Magic was sitting with a cup of tea reading the Daily Mail.

"Where is he, Magic?"

"He went to the toilet about five or so minutes ago."

"What, and you didn't follow him? Bloody hell Magic, this isn't good."

They both ran up the stairs shouting for Block. The bathroom door was blocked so Smarty kicked the door down. Mark Block was on the floor writhing about with what looked like a litre of sodium hypochlorite empty next to him.

"Mark, Mark," Smarty said repeatedly. By now Gammon was there.

"What the bloody hell happened?"

"John, never mind that, we need an ambulance urgent."

"Magic, sort it."

"Yes Sir."

It took twenty minutes for the ambulance and paramedics to arrive. While they waited Gammon read Magic the riot act, informing him there would be severe consequences.

"Will he survive, lads?"

"Can't say DI Gammon, but if he has had that full bottle the chances are he will have severely disabled his internal organs which have started shutting down now."

Series Three
Book Three
in the John Gammon Detective Series

The Ambulance left Poppy Mill at great speed.

Wally arrived and asked if the officers would leave the scene for fear of too much contamination.

"Ok team, back to Bixton."

On the way back Gammon informed DCI Dirk of what happened. Dirk was fuming.

"I want Sergeant Magic in my office when you arrive back at Bixton, and I want you as lead officer on the case to be in with him. He can bring his Police Federation rep with him also if he wishes."

Gammon told Magic. He knew that if DCI told him to ensure the Police Federation Rep was in attendance, it wasn't good.

They arrived back and Tim Baker from Micklock police station was there as Magic

BODY PARTS

had contacted him. Gammon knew Tim quite well so had a quick word before they all went up to DCI Dirk's office

Dirk was in no mood to muck about.

"My report Sergeant Magic, says you were sat drinking tea and reading a newspaper while the assailant went to the bathroom, and quite possible committed suicide. The evidence found by the team quite clearly shows Mark Block's involvement in the murder of Sally Darnell. You deemed it acceptable to allow him the freedom to wander round the house."

"DCI Dirk, my colleague is dreadfully sorry for his actions and assures me he won't ever do anything like that again."

"Try telling that to Mr and Mrs Darnell Tim, who now bury their only daughter, and nobody will be punished for her death."

"You are clearly an officer Sergeant Magic, that has been promoted beyond his capabilities. From today you will work the day shift as PC Magic. Sergeant Warren Beeney will be transferred at his request to Micklock Police. Have you anything to say?"

Magic stood up, "I am truly sorry, Sir."

Dirk just showed them the door but held Gammon back.

"I think that was fair John, don't you?"

"We all make mistakes Sir, but I do think he is lucky to still be in a job."

"It actually fell right to be honest. Beeney came to see me this morning saying there was a vacancy at Micklock, and that where he lives, so it would suit with no travelling. If that hadn't have happened, I would have bombed him out of the force, John."

BODY PARTS

"I understand Sir. Magic can be a bit off the wall at times, but he is a down to earth copper."

"Then he will be suited on the front desk dealing with the public."

Gammon could see there was no persuading DCI Dirk, so he let the matter drop.

"While you are here John, the press boys want to talk."

Again, Gammon thought, always me never the DCI.

"They are setting up at Bixton Place Hotel for the evening news. I would like you and DI Smarty to attend. I have been summoned to London, they want to know how a suspect was left alone to commit suicide."

Gammon didn't feel too bad when Dirk said about London. Gammon left Dirk's office and told DI smarty the good news.

"Oh brilliant, me and you are the ones about to get a right royal grilling, John."

"We can take it, mate."

BODY PARTS

CHAPTER TWO

At 5.30pm they headed for Bixton Palace Hotel and the assumed grilling from the press boys. The room held about three hundred. When Gammon and Smarty took to the stage the flashes were going crazy. Smarty estimated there was actually more than three hundred crammed into the room, with journalists and locals.

Gammon and Smarty sat as the first hand went up.

"Andy Nixon, Sky News. The public were led to believe that the poisonings in the Peak District were over and done with, yet we have another one with Sally Darnell and the suspect committing suicide. Why did you lead the public to believe they were safe?"

Series Three
Book Three
in the John Gammon Detective Series

Gammon adjusted the microphone in front of him and cleared his throat.

"It was never me, or my colleagues at Bixton Police, intention to misguide anybody. We were quite sure that the cult which originally carried out the atrocities was now defunct. Mark Block had been on our radar for the initial suspects."

"Kevin Glute, BBC News. If you suspected him, why wasn't he arrested?"

Smarty then spoke.

"You can't just arrest people if we have no credible evidence, and until we did have there was very little we could do. But as soon as we thought we were correct we raided Mr Block's house."

"Bob House, Central News. Can DI Gammon explain to the good people of Derbyshire why police officers were seen celebrating at a local hostelry for cracking the case about the poisoners, when in fact they hadn't? Does DI Gammon think this is correct behaviour?"

Gammon stood up.

"Who did you say you were?"

"Bob House, Central News."

"Ok Mr House. May I ask how long you have been a reporter?"

"Yes, I was twelve years with the Sun Newspaper group, four years with the Telegraph, and I have worked for Central News now for eighteen months."

"Quite impressive Mr House. During that time did you and your colleagues ever celebrate the result you had been working on for some months?"

"Occasionally. What has this got to do with the question, Mr Gammon?"

"Our team at Bixton are all hard working totally dedicated officers, and yes if we have a result that saves lives, we celebrate. I believe that you were involved in an incident with four colleagues when you worked at a newspaper, where a young lady sued two of your colleagues for rape after a night out celebrating with yourself."

"What's your point, Gammon?"

"My point Sir, is my officers work long hours with true dedication, and yes we will celebrate if we get a result like we did and have over many years. But it is always with a measure of knowledge we are serving police officers and therefore conduct ourselves correctly. So, in answer to your question I would ask you if you and your colleagues conduct yourselves correctly?"

The whole room laughed, and the next guy stood up.

"John Kay, Micklock Mercury. Mr Gammon, we all hope that this is the end of the tragic sect and its actions for these people, but I have been informed by a source that we have another murder in our community. Could you enlighten us about this please?"

"All I can say Mr Kay, at this time, is we have a suspicious death of a young man which we are investigating."

"Ok everybody, I am sure you can appreciate we are very busy, goodnight."

Gammon gestured to Smarty and they left the room.

Once in the car Gammon told Smarty that first thing in the morning they needed to go to Muscles Gym in Cramford to question them about Alan Hewitt.

"Are you coming for a quick beer with me, Dave?"

"Best not John, drop me at the station. Missus has got Slimming World tonight, so we always have a Chinese after she has weighed in."

"Not sure that helps, Dave," and Gammon laughed.

"It's her one treat of the week mate. She has lost eleven pounds in eight weeks."

John dropped Dave Smarty at the station to pick up his car and left for the Spinning Jenny. On the way John's mobile rang. It wasn't a number he recognised but thought he best answer it.

"John, hi. It's Fleur, how are you?"

"Fleur, where have you been? We go months without contact."

"Listen, forget that John. I am coming to Derbyshire for a week on holiday, but I can't stop at yours. Is there anywhere you can recommend?"

"I know Jim and Lisa Tink who own the farm at Clough Dale, just down from

BODY PARTS

Swinster. They have a beautiful place called Cambridge Lodge. Do you want me give Lisa a ring or check their website first?"

"Give her a ring, but what is the website? Be nice to have a look, John."

"When are you coming?"

"I arrive Saturday at East Midlands at 8.00am from Charles De Gaulle. Can you pick me up?"

"Yes, of course I will, and I can't wait to see you, Fleur."

"Aww thanks John, don't forget to send me the website of your friend's place."

"I will get straight on it. See you Saturday."

John called Lisa to ask about availability for a week from Saturday.

"You are so lucky John, we are usually fully booked but a woman just cancelled. Her husband isn't well."

"What's your website as well, Lisa?"

"It's www.cloughviewfarmbandb.co.uk."

John knew Lisa and Jim quite well. Jim's father had farmed for many years before Jim started farming, but he decided a few years back to start his own business I-Fabrication, so that was his forte now. Lisa ran a B & B at the farm and also the rental of Cambridge Lodge.

The accommodation was booked under his half-sister's name, Fleur Dubois, so that no suspicion arose. John carried onto the Spinning Jenny. In the car park he texted Fleur the website for Cambridge Lodge.

Kev was in his customary place at the bar in a white shirt and red dickie bow. He always looked immaculate, a real mine host John's mum used to say.

"Evening lad, how are you?"

"I'm good Kev, quiet tonight?"

"We have been really busy this afternoon. Must have had sixty walkers for meals and drinks. Poor Jane was rushed off her feet, weren't you duck?"

Jane Halzimmer smiled as much to say as always.

"Pour a Pedigree for John, love, and put it on my tab please."

John started to tell Kev that Fleur was coming over for a week.

"What about you and Saron, John?"

"I haven't seen her John. We are still close, but I don't think she is really over the wedding thing."

"Can't blame her lad."

"I know Kev, that's why she must never find out about Anka Emily, or she will never forgive me for that."

"Your secret is safe with me, mate."

John was thinking of calling it a night when Steve came in with the landlady from the Star at Puddle Dale, Imogen Elliot.

"Thought I might find you here, mate."

"I'm not hard to find, Steve."

"Pretty much a creature of habit, eh John. You remember Imogen from the Star at Puddle Dale."

"Was your hair a different colour last time I saw you, Imogen?"

"Yes, it was John, but I fancied a copper top look."

"Well it certainly suits you."

"Back off," Steve said. "She is my date for the night," and he laughed.

BODY PARTS

Kev was sitting with his mouth open wide to see Steve with a new woman.

"Now then Kev, how are we mate?"

"Not as well as you lad, I don't think."

"Imogen, this is Kev. Of course, you have met John."

Nice to meet you Kev. I have got the Star at Puddle Dale."

"Yes, I did hear you were enjoying it."

"Hard work Kev, but I love the interaction with the customers."

"Well if you can get Saturday off would be nice to see you and Steve. I have got Pants On Yer Head Bob and the Calculators who are a sixties/seventies group. Should be a good night."

"I will see what I can do Kev. Thanks for telling us."

John noted the word 'us' implying this was more than a first date.

Steve seemed really happy. John was pleased that his mate was coping, as it must have been so hard. That was something else he wanted to talk to Fleur about - bloody Brian Lund.

John decided to have an early night. Steve had left at 10.00pm and Kev said he was tired. John called it a night and was back home by 10.30pm. John opened the kitchen door and picked up his post. The first few letters were companies wanting him to take out a credit card and a time share in Tenerife. Then the next letter had a typed envelope addressed to Mr John Gammon. John was always careful opening post. Inside was a typed letter. John sat at the kitchen table and began to read.

'Dear John

BODY PARTS

I see you found my victim Alan Hewitt which is good, he can have a proper burial but it doesn't stop there.

My work won't be done until I have you involved and your lovely girl Saron. I was surprised you did what you did to her, with her being a stunner and all that.

Anyway that day is a fair way off so until we actually do meet I promise to keep you busy.

Frank Stein (Woody)'

What sort of nutcase signs his name? It can't be his real name John thought. By now it was almost midnight, so John called it a night. He carefully put the letter in a plastic scene of crime bag to give to Wally in the morning.

The following morning John felt quite excited that Fleur was coming for a week.

Series Three
Book Three
in the John Gammon Detective Series

He decided to take the Monday and Tuesday off so he could show her round a bit. Once at the station Gammon informed Dirk of his plan. Rather than saying about his sister he just said he fancied a couple of days off.

Dirk seemed disinterested. He said he had pretty much had the stuffing knocked out of him in London over the bleach case, and he hoped that was it now. Gammon reminded him about Alan Hewitt, the guy who died from having his arm removed. Dirk's stock answer was it could have been drug related, and the body dumped in the Peak District. Gammon couldn't be bothered to tell him Hewitt lived locally. He thought he clearly hadn't even read the scene of crime report.

"Ok Sir, best get on."

BODY PARTS

Dirk just smiled, and Gammon left the office thinking whatever was said in London the writing was on the wall for DCI Dirk. He had seen it so many times since he arrived at Bixton.

Gammon went down to Wally to give him the letter from what he thought was a fictitious Frank Stein. Wally rolled his eyes.

"Bloody hell John, I am snowed under at the minute. Angie is off sick, and Trevor has gone to see his daughter in Australia for six weeks, so you will have to be patient mate."

"Not a problem, Wally. I know you will have answers by the morning," and Gammon wandered off smiling to himself, hearing Wally mumbling as he left.

Gammon went back to his office and called Smarty in.

"Think we should go to Muscles Gym in Cramford Dave. Let's see if this guy had any enemies."

"Sounds good to me, let me grab my coat."

Cramford was a tidy little village famed for its association with Sir Richard Arkwright. It claimed to have the first industrialised factory and was now used by the Arkwright Society to tell people the story. It uncannily had three pubs still operating, and the houses were quite often three storeys. Arkwright was the first entrepreneur to use people for out-work and the top storey was used for this purpose.

Since those days it had become a thriving village. Although only small it boasted two chip shops, three pubs, a club, a famed bookstore, a butcher, tea rooms and numerous other small enterprises. Muscles Gym was housed in a former mill just outside Cramford.

Gammon and Smarty pulled up outside the converted mill and could see the entrance to Muscles. They went in and a massive guy who called himself Snake shook their hands, which made Smarty wince as it was like a vice grip.

"How can I help you two gentlemen?"

They showed Snake their warrant cards.

"Are you the owner, Mr Snake?"

"Just call me Snake. I am part owner."

"Is the other owner here?"

"No, she lives in Spain, it's my ex-wife."

"Oh, I see."

"So, what is this about Mr Gammon?"

"Have you got an office where we can talk?"

The office was in the top floor of the converted mill, and they threaded their way through muscle bound men and women working out.

"Makes you feel in adequate, John."

"Speak for yourself."

"You look like you could both do with a bit of muscle," Snake commented.

Once in the small office Gammon's eyes were everywhere. There were tacky body building medals and tubs of muscle building powder stacked up in one corner.

"We are investigating the murder of Alan Hewitt, who I believe was a member of the gym here, Snake?"

"Yes, rum do about Alan, nice lad, could be a bit of a hot head mind."

"Was he taking steroids?"

"I can't possibly comment Mr Gammon. What these lads do in their own time is entirely up to them. I run a clean gym here."

Smarty smiled.

"Do you know of anybody that might have wished Mr Hewitt dead?"

"Well it's a bit harsh, but not everyone liked him. Not enough to kill him I wouldn't have thought, Mr Gammon."

"So, he had no real enemies here at the gym?"

"There was one of members who did have a go at him a few weeks back."

"What was his name?"

"They call him Foggy."

"What his is correct name?"

"Hang on, let me look."

Snake got up and looked in the old filing cabinet.

"Here it is, Peter Scarthin."

"Why do they call him Foggy?"

"Apparently he is a bit Tim, Tim nice but Dim."

"Is he here now?"

"No, I haven't seen him for a few weeks, possibly since that row with Alan Hewitt."

"Have you got an address for Mr Scarthin."

"It says here he lives at Lavender Farm in Pommie, but that's all I have Mr Smarty."

"Ok, well thanks Snake, we will be in touch."

"Don't forget I will do you a good deal on gym membership you two."

Gammon and Smarty smiled as they walked away. Snake looked fearsome with all his tattoos piercings and muscle, but he seemed a genuinely nice guy.

BODY PARTS

They drove off to the village of Pommie. Gammon stopped at the butchers and Smarty popped into ask directions.

"Up this side lane, John."

The lane had big tractor ruts in it and a Landrover would have struggled. John took it carefully and they arrived at a rundown farm. Gammon wasn't happy. He got out of the car straight into a big dollop of cow muck.

"What a bloody shit hole, Dave."

"Do you think he lives here, John? It hardly looks habitable. Look, some slates are missing off the roof."

Suddenly a big guy with a black wool hat on appeared waving a shotgun.

"What do you bloody want? This is private property, be off with you."

"We are police officers, Mr Scarthin."

Smarty gently took out his warrant card not wanting to spook the guy.

"Put the gun down Mr Scarthin, we mean you no harm."

Scarthin lowered the double barrel shot gun.

"What dos tha want wi me?"

"Just a few questions, Mr Scarthin. Can we come inside?"

"If tha wants."

Scarthin showed them into the kitchen. The sink was full of dirty pots. The curtains looked like they had never been washed. Luckily Scarthin didn't offer them a drink.

"Is this your permanent residence, Mr Scarthin?"

"If tha means do I live here? Yes, I do."

"We are investigating the death of Mr Alan Hewitt. How well did you know Mr Hewitt?"

BODY PARTS

"I worked with him years back at the toy factory, and then when I joined the gym I would see him there?"

"We believe you had a falling out at the gym, is that correct?"

"Yes, he is a bloody big head, loved himself as my dad would say, he is ten bob champagne Charlie."

"So, it's safe to say you didn't like him."

"Can't say I disliked him, just tried to avoid him."

"Why was that?"

Well when I worked at the toy factory I used to assemble the dolls. Sometimes I would catch the light beam that stopped you going into the line while it was assembling the heads. He would have to come and reset the line, which made him angry and he would call me names."

"What sort of names?"

"He would shout Scruffy from the Ugly Tree does it again."

"Did this make you mad?"

"Not really, just it wasn't nice. But I don't think many people liked him he was so big headed."

"So where do you work now?"

"Nowhere. Since the toy factory shut my dad left me this place, so I can survive on selling the odd cow here and there."

"Ok Mr Scarthin, we may need to speak again."

"That's ok, Mr Gammon."

Scarthin showed them out.

"Bloody hell John, what a shit hole. Did you notice how he lost his Derbyshire accent when we started talking about Hewitt. He is not as thick as he is making out John."

BODY PARTS

"But be honest Dave, do you believe he killed Hewitt?"

"Guess not John, don't think he has it in him."

"What was that woman's name that found the body? She said she worked at the toy factory, didn't she?"

"Yes, Stella Watkins from Dilley Dale. Come on let's go and see her."

They drove to Stella Watkins at Dilley Dale and luckily she was in. Gammon knocked on the door and Stella answered it.

"Oh hello, Mr Gammon."

"Could we have a quick word, Stella?"

"Of course, come on in. I have just baked a pineapple ring cake I, am sure you and Mr Smarty would like a piece of that with a tea."

"Very good of you Stella. Could I have a strong black coffee though please?"

"Of course, Mr Gammon. Are you the same Mr Smarty?"

"No, good ole Rosie Lee for me Stella."

They sat in the neat living room. There were pictures of children on a beach and a couple taken some years earlier at work with workmates.

Stella came back with a piece of pineapple cake for Gammon and Smarty draped in thick clotted cream.

"Wow, this is lovely Stella."

"Well I live on my own but have always like baking. I still do it but take most of it to coffee mornings either at Church or the Women's Institute."

"Blimey I wished my wife could bake like this Stella."

Stella coloured up at Smarty's comment.

"Now how can I help you?"

BODY PARTS

"You said when we last spoke to you, that you knew Alan Hewitt when you worked at the toy factory?"

"I worked there for forty five years, straight from school until I retired with ill health. I was the bear stuffer supervisor. I loved it Mr Gammon, and was devastated when the doctor said all the dust from the bear fillings were causing havoc with my breathing."

"How many people did it employ?"

"There must have been over five hundred when I started. We were like a big happy family. We would have days out to Skegness and Blackpool and the owners paid for everything."

"Who were the owners?"

"Mr Jeffery and Mr Malcolm. Sorry, they were brothers, their surname was

Ross. Lovely men really cared for their workforce."

"The last ten years were different. Mr Malcolm was killed in a car accident and Mr Jeffery was never the same. I am sure he died of a broken heart. The factory was left to Mr Malcolm's two children, Jonathon and Bunty. Neither of them were interested, and poor Mr Jeffery hadn't been in the ground five minutes when it was sold. The new owners cut the staff back to just one hundred and fifty, and put some new-fangled machinery in, but it was never the same. They lost some big contracts. I mean we used to make the Action Man figures, Barbie and Ken, Paddington teddies, the list goes on and on."

"But Alan Hewitt, you hardly knew?"

"That's correct. I was retiring when he started. I knew him to say hello to but that's all."

"Did you know a Peter Scarthin?"

"Oh yes, everybody loved Peter; nice man probably a bit on the slow side so some took the mickey. He was good at his job, he worked in the assembly department on the lines."

"You don't think Peter has anything to do with the case, do you Mr Gammon? He wouldn't hurt a fly."

"Just following a line of enquiry, Stella."

"Well I can tell you now he wasn't as slow as people thought before my daughter went to Australia."

Stella picked the couple of pictures with kids on a beach.

"She lives in Sydney, been there a lot of years now, would never come back she said. The grandkids have a great life. Sorry I digress, Peter helped my Lucy and her husband Duncan pack all their things to ship to Australia. Do you know he wouldn't have a penny for doing it, that's the kind hearted lad he is. Does he still live in Pommie? I heard he was farming his dad's place."

John thought better of commenting on what a mess it was so he just answered, "Yes."

"Can you think of anybody else who may have wanted Hewitt dead?"

"Like I say, I hardly knew him Mr Gammon."

"Ok Stella, thank you so much for your help, it's been interesting, and that cake was lovely."

Stella flashed a contented smile at Gammon as she showed them out.

BODY PARTS

"Think we can count Scarthin out of our enquiries, Dave."

"Yeah, seems like he was well liked. Maybe being up there at that farm on his own is making him twitchy, hence the greeting with the shotgun."

"Probably so Dave. Ok, let's head back."

Gammon had only been back five minutes when Dirk called him in.

"What do you want to do about Magic's replacement, John?"

"Not really sure what we have now, Sir. Why?"

"Oh, just that Ackbourne DCI mentioned that he had an officer that has been with them four years. He is living in Swinster and fancied a crack at a DI's job here at Bixton."

"Get him, let's have a look. What's his name, Sir?"

"John Winnipeg."

"Great name, DS Winnipeg eh, Sir."

"I suppose it is. Are you free to chat with the guy say 10.00am?"

"I think so, Sir."

"Ok John, I will arrange it for then. I don't think it needs us both, if you like him get him started as soon as possible."

"Ok Sir will do."

Gammon left Dirk's office and noticed it was now 4.30pm so he grabbed a quick coffee and sat at his desk. His phone rang.

"Yes, PC Magic."

Magic didn't sound too happy in his new position.

"You have a call from the Tow'd Man."

"Ok put it through, Magic."

"Hello."

BODY PARTS

"Oh, hi John, it's Saron, how are you? Just thought I would give you a call. Bob and Cheryl were in last night and he said they are doing a show at the Spinning Jenny with Bob opening. I just wondered if you fancied taking me?"

Fancied taking her! John thought that's an understatement.

"Yeah, I will pick you up at 7.45pm tomorrow night then."

"Ok John, that will be nice."

John sat at his desk thinking how odd women were. One minute they are talking, next they will walk past you, then when you least expect it they fancy going out. With his day ending well John called it a night and decided on a Doreen take away from the spinning Jenny.

It was a beautiful night as John set off from Bixton. He took the winding roads all the way to Swinster and the Spinning Jenny. There were a lot of what looked like walkers in the beer garden, which Kev always kept immaculate with beautiful hanging baskets of every colour imaginable.

In the bar there was nobody except Kev behind the bar.

"Hello mate, how are you?"

"Good Kev."

"Are you coming Saturday night, should be a good do mate."

"Yeah, I'm coming with Saron."

He only just got the words out of his mouth when he realised that Fleur was up on Saturday.

"Oh crap."

"What's the matter?"

BODY PARTS

"Well Saron asked if I wanted to bring her to this thing Saturday night and I said I would, but forgot Fleur is coming for a week's holiday starting Saturday."

"Bring them both."

"Do you reckon I can pull it off, Kev? If I had asked Saron it would have been different, but with her asking me she probably doesn't want Fleur playing the gooseberry."

"You think too deep lad, invite them both."

"Right, pour me a Pedigree mate and I'll call Saron."

Saron's mobile rang three times and eventually she answered.

"Saron Tow'd Man, how can I help?"

"Hey sweetheart, it's John."

Series Three
Book Three
in the John Gammon Detective Series

"Sorry John, just instinctively answered and didn't look who was calling. You are not calling to cancel tomorrow, are you?"

"No, nothing like that but Fleur is coming for a week's holiday and I wondered if she wanted to come would you mind her tagging along?"

"No, that's fine John. It will be nice to meet her at last and have a catch up. Still picking me up?"

"Yes, sweetheart, see you tomorrow."

"I'll have to go John, we have a party of twenty eight in for evening meal."

"Ok, bye," and John hung up.

"Sorted Kev."

"See, that wasn't that difficult, was it?"

"You were right, as usual."

Kev sat opposite John behind the bar.

"So, young Lineman has a new woman in his life then, John?"

BODY PARTS

"He hasn't told me."

"Well they looked like an item the other night. I think I must be old fashioned, but do you think it's a bit soon after Jo, John?"

"Steve can't change what happened and he has had a rough time mate, so if he is finding happiness with Imogen, then why not I say?"

"Suppose you are right."

"Might ask Doreen for a take-out, Kev."

"No, sit there. She is trying out some dishes and I am her guinea-pig, so you might as well help me. She will do extra if she knows her blue eyed boy is chief tester."

"Blue eyed boy?" and John laughed.

Kev nipped to tell Doreen in the kitchen and he came back with six of a new starter.

"Try these, mate."

"What are they?"

"A small potato cake with chives wrapped in cabbage and bread crumbs and deep fried. Oh, and the dip is mustard mayonnaise."

"Wow Kev, these are bloody lovely. I could eat all six."

"You would do so at your peril," Kev said and laughed making his red dickie bow bounce up and down as he chuckled.

Next out was another potato croquette, but this time it was potato, black pudding in light beer batter with a sweet chilli dip.

"Bloody hell Kev, pleased I called tonight."

"She is bringing a miniature main course out for us to try next."

Twenty minutes and another pint later Doreen appeared with what she called her Lead Miners stripped steak. This was sirloin steak cut into strips with onions, button mushrooms, Hittington Stilton, cream and celery. With the dish she had made baby roast potatoes, chopped brussell sprouts with streaky bacon in a small cranberry jus, bay carrots and kale.

"Doreen, you should go on Master-chef. You would walk it; every dish was fabulous."

"Thank you, John, I knew you would appreciate. I'm not sure that bloody lummox in his red dickie bow appreciates good food, although you wouldn't know it looking at the size of him."

"Harsh, my dear."

"Feeling harsh Kevin. I thought you were mowing the field today?"

"Too wet, my lovely."

"Likely bloody story," and she wandered off back to the kitchen with the empty plates.

"In trouble again, mate?"

"I'm always in trouble. She loves me really," and he laughed again.

"Can't do a pint mate, I'm full. Let's have a brandy a-piece, my shout John."

"Thank you very much."

John sat on his stool feeling like a contented kitten; lovely food, now a brandy. Does life get any better he thought?

John decided to call it a night. Kev said he wasn't going to be late with the group and that on tomorrow night.

John arrived at his cottage and opened the door there was just one letter on the floor with a typed address on it. John was pretty sure who this was from.

He carefully opened the letter and read it.

'I am guessing it will be evening when you read this so I hope you have had a

*great day. The reason for the letters I send
you will be revealed when I have done what
I have set out to do.*

*I don't like calling people victims so if
you don't mind I will call the people
involved INVOLVERS. The reason for this
is they are involved in a dream I have.*

*I write to you to tell you of Larry Bailey
he can be found at Hittington fishing lake
by the Bailiff's cabin.*

*Sadly he is dead but it is best because I
have his legs.*

*Anyway will keep you informed along the
way.*

*Bye for now John
Frank Stein'*

John rang DCI Dirk immediately and
told him of the letter. His typical DCI stock
answer was, "Then you better get over
there right away, John."

Series Three
Book Three
in the John Gammon Detective Series

There was no commitment from him to go also. John was just told to get a team and Wally over there and keep him informed.

John rang Smarty.

"Have you been out, Dave?"

"No mate, why? It's almost midnight."

John proceeded to tell Dave about the letter and the body and he said he would get Wally, Scooper, Milton and Lee to the scene.

John quickly dived in the shower after putting the letter in a sealed bag to give to Wally. Smarty arrived about forty minutes after the telephone conversation and they headed for the crime scene the fishing lake at Hittington.

"I used to fish here with my brother all through the summer holidays. I remember old Mr Dalton would catch us and try and chase us, but we were like greyhounds in the day, Dave."

"Always been a maverick then, John." Gammon laughed.

It was a short walk from the car park and John could see Wally's tent as they got out of the car. Milton, Scooper and Lee arrived.

"Sorry about this gang but we have another victim, this time apparently the killer has taken his legs."

"What is wrong with this sicko, John?"

"Sadly that is the world today, mate. We aren't all normal, Wally."

"You don't have to tell me, mate."

"Can we have something for 9.00am Monday, mate?"

"Will do my best John. Lucky it's you though."

Gammon smiled.

There was nobody about and the body hadn't been disturbed so Gammon called it a night. Smarty took him back. They made their way to Gammon's cottage.

"John, what was the name the killer is calling himself?"

"Bloody Frank Stein."

"Don't you get it mate? FRANKENSTEIN."

"Bloody hell Dave, you are right. He is making a monster out of body parts. Well done, mate."

"Well, it just came to me, John."

Feeling quite pleased with himself, he had always looked up to Gammon, as did most of the team. Smarty dropped Gammon off at home and John made his way straight to bed.

BODY PARTS

The following morning John was up early. He rang Lisa Tink to check everything was ok for Fleur. Lisa said all was good and the key would be under the plant pot.

John grabbed a quick coffee then headed for East Midlands. He felt excited that his half-sister would be with him for a week. He was also mindful of the latest murder and although he had booked Monday and Tuesday off to be with Fleur, he had decided to go in for Wally's results on the latest killing.

John arrived at the airport, parked his car and headed for arrivals. The flight from Charles De Gaulle airport was delayed by ten minutes but eventually a radiant Fleur came through with her case. The pair hugged for what seemed an age,

Series Three
Book Three
in the John Gammon Detective Series

"I have found a lovely place for you, Cambridge Lodge with fabulous views, Fleur. Why could you not stop at mine?"

"Well John, I am here for a holiday, but I also have to work, so please don't ask. I can't have anything coming back to you.

"Ok I won't ask and maybe you will tell me."

"So how are you and what happened to your wedding day?"

"Well, me being me, I slept with a woman on the eve of my wedding day."

"Sacra bleu," Fleur said in a thick French accent. "Really?"

"Not proud of it."

"So, are you with her now?"

"No, she became pregnant and went home. I am the father of a little girl, Anka Emily."

BODY PARTS

"Wow John, no half measures with you. So that's why the marriage didn't happen."

"Well I ended up working on the day of my marriage. To cut a long story short I had an accident heading to my wedding so then everything came out."

"So, Saron has nothing to do with you now?"

"No, we are still good friends but can't see us getting back. I don't think she can forgive me. Which brings me to tonight, I am taking Saron to the Spinning Jenny to hear a comedian and there is a group. Saron would love to meet you."

"Well if it's ok, I would like that."

"So where is my accommodation, John? I looked at the website and it looked fabulous."

Series Three
Book Three
in the John Gammon Detective Series

"It's the next village down from Swinster where we are going tomorrow night."

"Can't wait to see this place, the reviews on Trip Advisor were excellent. They all say what a lovely couple they are who run it and how clean the accommodation is."

"Yes, I think I chose well. Jim and Lisa have a great reputation and they say Lisa ensures everybody who stays wants to come back. I guess the Trip Advisor reports are testimony to how well it's run."

"What a great name, Cambridge Lodge. I wonder why it is called that."

"Don't know Fleur, but I am sure Lisa will know. I have booked a couple of days off with you on Monday and Tuesday, but I need to go in to work for a couple of hours on Monday."

BODY PARTS

"Not a problem, come down for breakfast on Sunday and we can have a chat and I will explain a few things to you." John followed the small lane off the main road into Clough Dale. The lane was about a quarter of a mile long until they arrived at Cambridge Lodge. Fleur got out of the car and was awestruck.

"John, this is fabulous, what views."

"Yeah, pretty impressive."

John grabbed the key and opened the picture window door.

"Wow, look at this Fleur."

"That's a nice touch John, look Lisa has left a note with some flowers."

'Dear Fleur

Jim and I hope you enjoy your stay at Cambridge Lodge. You will find eggs, tea, coffee, a small locally sourced loaf and some croissants to get you started.

Series Three
Book Three
in the John Gammon Detective Series

You have my number if you need anything, please don't hesitate to call me. Have a lovely holiday

Best Wishes

Lisa and Jim x'

"How wonderful John. I have stayed in some of the best hotels in the world and this level of commitment to customers is way beyond anything I have seen."

"Well I heard it was good but never thought it was this good, to be honest Fleur."

"You chose well, brother."

It felt incredibly strange hearing Fleur call him brother. He really hardly knew her but was determined this time he would get to know her well.

"Listen Fleur, I should probably just pop in to work for an hour or so."

"Ok John, that is fine."

BODY PARTS

CHAPTER THREE

John left Fleur as she wandered round Cambridge Lodge extolling the wonders of the place.

It was 11.10pm when John arrived at Bixton. Magic was on the front desk reading a book which he quickly dropped when he saw Gammon come through the front door.

"Afternoon Sir, everything ok?"

Gammon was still annoyed with Magic although he thought it was harsh the treatment DCI Dirk had metered out.

"Wally, is he in?"

"Yes Sir, two of them are in, Wally and Vicki Lodge."

Gammon swept past the front desk and headed to forensics.

"How are you doing, Wally?"

"Bloody hell, John, gives us chance."

"I know mate."

"I will have all the results by Monday. What I can tell you is, he is male about thirty five years old and a diabetic."

"Ok Wally, I am going to check that name from the letter on the Police records."

"Before you ask John, we haven't had chance to check the letter yet."

"Understand, mate."

Gammon sat at his desk and put in the name Larry Bailey. There was a police record for indecent exposure four years earlier. He had been given a suspended sentence so there was no doubt who he was. Gammon decided to inform his wife, so he headed for Cramford.

Number four, Hickey Road had been a former lock keeper's cottage for the old

canal which had now been turned into a
tourist attraction.

Gammon knocked on the door. A woman
answered. She looked in her mid-fifties,
had a cigarette dangling from her mouth
and her appearance was quite unkempt.

"What do you want? We aren't a bloody
café."

Gammon showed his warrant card.

"May I come in, Mrs Bailey."

"I suppose so," she said dragging her
feet in a slovenly manner.

"What do you want?"

"When was the last time you saw your
husband?"

"What's he done now? Last time it was
nicking bloody lead off church roof."

"I'm afraid your husband has been
murdered, Mrs Bailey."

"No bloody loss to me."

Gammon could not believe what he was hearing.

"He was never the same after he got finished at the toy factory in Dilley Dale."

"Your husband worked at the toy factory?"

"Yes, that's where we met. I was in charge of the canteen."

That conjured up all-sorts of images in Gammon's head.

"I used to give him an extra scoop of mash or extra slice of roast beef. Then he asked me out. He was a different man then."

"In what way Mrs Bailey?"

"Well four years back he got done for indecent exposure and looking back it all started then. He would go out drinking and not come back for days on end. We had no marriage and after that we just lived together."

The cigarette in her mouth had almost burnt down to nothing so she lit a new one with the embers left and popped that in her mouth. What a disgusting woman Gammon thought.

"Did he have any enemies?"

"That's all he had, because he had no friends, Mr Gammon."

"What do you mean?"

"Well at the toy factory his job was to ensure the lines had all they needed for assembling the dolls and the teddies."

"So, what was the problem?"

He would go down into the boiler house and sleep, so people hated him. They wouldn't tell the Manager they just fetched their own stuff. I didn't know any of this and felt sorry for him. My biggest mistake."

"Any children in the marriage?"

"You are bloody joking. I think he only ever touched me three times in nine years. Whoever did this has done me a favour, Mr Gammon."

"I have to ask this. Would you like somebody to sit with you?"

"What to watch me celebrate? I have a big insurance policy I took out when we were married. Bloody set me up for life that will."

"Ok Mrs Bailey, but you will need to pop into Bixton to identify the body."

"With pleasure, Mr Gammon," and she laughed.

Gammon left Bailey with a big grin on her face. He thought he had seen most things in his job, but this cow took the biscuit. On the way back he phoned Fleur, but it just rang so he thought she had perhaps gone for a walk or something.

John arrived back at his cottage thinking that he had two dismembered bodies and only one slight suspect in Peter Scarthin from Pommie. He decided to forget work for the weekend and concentrate on a night out with Saron and Fleur.

It was 3.30pm so John decided to nip and see Saron. He arrived at the Tow'd Man and Saron was just getting out of her car.

"Hi John, you ok?"

John felt a glow from within for Saron to be so welcoming, maybe there was a chance.

"Are you coming in for a coffee?"

"Yes, that would be nice."

"Great, I'll show you my new dress I have bought for tonight."

They headed for Saron's apartment. John made them both a coffee and he waited while Saron changed into her new dress.

"What do you think, John?"

Saron stood radiant with her blonde hair cascading over her shoulders. Her dress was off the shoulder and was cream with a slight pale blue trim. She had white stockings and pale blue high heels to complement the look.

"You look fabulous, Saron.

He wanted to say gorgeous, but thought he best take things slowly.

"Come into my bedroom and unzip me please."

John followed Saron into her bedroom, his heart racing as he unzipped the dress touching her milky skin as the zip was brought down. Saron stepped out of the dress and hung it on the door. She then turned around and stood looking at John seductively. Her bright blue eyes were saying something to John as she twirled her blonde hair in her hand seductively.

"What are you waiting for, Mr Gammon?"

John held her slim body tightly to him and laid her on the bed in her white lingerie and stockings. He began kissing her neck, then working his way down her body. John slowly removed her underwear just leaving her stockings and pale blue shoes. Saron was breathless and John was the same. She kissed him everywhere then straddled on top of him and they made love and lust at the same time, before John could wait no longer. Saron screamed with ecstasy as his fullness made her shudder.

Series Three
Book Three
in the John Gammon Detective Series

It was all over, but they both knew at that point that nothing could ever be over with them.

Saron draped herself over John and cuddled into him. They both felt contentment. They woke with a start realising it was now 6.00pm.

"I best get back and get changed and showered. I will pick you up about 7.30pm, then we can get Fleur from Cambridge Lodge in Clough Dale."

"Thank you John, you don't know how much I have missed you."

"Me too, I am so sorry about the wedding."

Saron pressed her dainty finger to his mouth and said, "I will see you in a bit."

John left and arrived back at his cottage. He could hardly believe his luck with Saron. Maybe they could make it up, but should he be upfront about baby Anka Emily and chance losing Saron again? It was probably best to leave it for a while he thought.

John shaved and showered and headed back to pick Saron up. He had a quick half while he was waiting for Saron.

"Looking very dapper, John."

"Thanks Donna."

"Are you two working things out then?"

"I'm hoping that's the plan."

"Well I hope so, you make a lovely couple."

Saron came into the bar in the beautiful dress she had shown him earlier with a small ermine fur shawl to cover her shoulders.

"You ready, Mr Gammon?"

"I certainly am, pretty lady."

Series Three
Book Three
in the John Gammon Detective Series

"Guessing I will be late Donna."

"No worries, you got your key?"

"Yes."

"Ok, I will lock up. Have a great night."

Saron waved and they left.

"I'm a bit nervous meeting Fleur, John."

"She is lovely Saron, she really is."

As they turned up the drive to Cambridge Lodge they could see Fleur on the patio on her mobile.

She finished her call and got in John's car.

"You must be Saron, I have heard so much about you," she said in her thick French accent.

"Likewise Fleur, John has told me loads about you."

They arrived at the Spinning Jenny and John introduced Fleur to Shelley and Jack,

BODY PARTS

Bob and Cheryl, Carol Lestar who was with Tracey Rodgers.

"No Steve tonight, Tracey?"

"Yes, he is coming. I think he is bringing Imogen from the Star at Puddle Dale."

The drinks were flowing and Saron and Fleur were really getting on well. It was now 9.00pm and Kev introduced Bob.

"Ladies and Gentlemen, let's have a big hand for a local favourite, Pants on Yer Head Bob."

The place erupted.

"Just a quick one for you. A bloke walks into a bar with a giraffe. He orders a double brandy for the giraffe and a pint for himself. Standing on a stool he gives the giraffe its brandy. The giraffe drinks it and promptly wobbles and falls over in front of the bar. Everybody coming to the bar had to climb over the giraffe. The man isn't concerned and finally finishes his pint before shouting to the landlord goodnight as he heads to the door. The landlord in a panic runs from behind the bar and stops the man. Sorry mate, but you can't leave that lying there, pointing at the giraffe. The man says it's not a lion, it's a giraffe."

Fleur didn't quite get the humour so Saron tried to explain. Bob was on for forty five minutes before finishing his act to a standing ovation.

Kev stood back up.

"Thanks Bob, brilliant as always and now Doreen as some spare knickers," as he picked up the pairs of knickers people had thrown on the stage in fun.

"Ok ladies and gents, a great local group are next for you. They have been together a few years. They work together and are all accountants and I am sure you all know the kind of music they play. So, a big hand for The Calculators.

The group when straight into a Searchers number Sugar and Spice. The dance floor was full. Saron and Fleur got up and John was standing at the bar when Tracey Rodgers came up to get a drink.

"Evening Mr Gammon, are you back with Saron?"

"Not sure yet. Where's Steve?"

"Apparently he is helping Imogen at the Star. Two staff haven't turned in so she can't come, and Steve said he would help out."

"How are you getting on with Imogen?"

"Yeah ok John, it's a bit difficult seeing Steve with her, you know after our Jo, but he needs to be happy."

"Is he still living at yours?"

"Not much now, he is always at Imogen's."

"Has he started on the rebuild?"

"No and from what he said a couple of nights back he probably thinks it was a bad idea."

"Well I did wonder, Tracey. He doesn't want to forget but he needs to move on."

The group finished their first song then sang The Communards 'Don't Leave me This Way'. The lead singer had a fantastic voice, as good as a professional.

"Hey Kev, what you drinking?"

"I'll have a pint of Lonely Hearts. It's a grand drink John."

"Best get one for me then as well."

Saron and Fleur never came off the dance floor.

"Saron seems very happy John. Are you two sorting things out?"

BODY PARTS

"I am hoping so."

"Well if you do, take some advice off a more mature man. Stop fishing when you have caught your supper, that's what my dad used to say."

"Just worried about the baby with Anouska, Kev."

"Your secret is safe with me lad."

"I know that, but what if I don't tell her and she finds out further down the line, then what?"

"Well I guess you have to decide that one lad and honesty is always the best policy."

By midnight there was Kev and Doreen, Jane Halzimmer who had worked the bar, Bob and Cheryl, Jack and Shelly Etchings, Sheba Filey and Phil Sterndale had also been out dancing, Saron and Fleur, John,

Carol Lestar and Jimmy Lowcee the pair had been helping Jane behind the bar.

"Right everyone, me and Doreen have an announcement to make."

"She's not pregnant, is she?" shouted Bob.

"No bloody way Bob," retorted Doreen.

"We wanted our closest friends to know first, but we have decided we are going to retire. So, we are putting the Spinning Jenny on the market next week."

"Aww, you can't do that, it won't be the same without Doreen's cooking and Kev's dickie bow behind the bar."

"Sorry Carol, we have thought long and hard and we have over twenty years here. I will say good years with great memories and good friends, that we feel it's now time to pass on the baton."

Shelley was a bit upset.

BODY PARTS

"Where are you going to?"

"We aren't sure yet Shelley. We have got the bungalow in the village which we think we might stop renting that and live there, but nothing decided yet though. Don't worry, I'm sure we will probably see more of you this side of the bar."

They all had a couple more drinks and recalled the fun they had over the years. John had arranged a taxi for Fleur and he told her would pop down the following morning and they could do something together. Jack and Shelley were getting the mini bus and they agreed to drop John and Saron at John's place.

One inside the cottage John made them a coffee while Saron went up to freshen up. He arrived with the coffees and Saron was fast asleep in his bed. He looked at her for a minute knowing in his heart of hearts this was the girl for him. He promised himself that if he got a second chance which was looking more likely then he would grab it with both hands this time.

He slipped between the sheets and held her she just murmured.

The following morning John woke to the smell of bacon. He slipped a sweatshirt on and his boxers and went downstairs. Saron was cooking bacon. John could not believe how Saron could look so beautiful in just his old sweatshirt.

"Blimey John, I was tired out with all that drink and dancing with Fleur, she really is lovely John."

"What did you say she did? She was a bit evasive when I asked her."

"She is something to do with French and British intelligence."

BODY PARTS

"Oh wow, any wonder she was coy," and Saron laughed.

John put his arms around Saron and kissed her.

"John, everything feels right when I'm with you, but this voice in my head keep saying you will hurt me again."

"I won't Saron. I want this more than anything."

"Let's just go slowly, John."

"Ok, if that's what you want."

They sat and had breakfast.

"I have arranged a taxi for 10.00am to drop me at the Tow'd Man. Do you want them to take you for your car?"

"Yeah, might as well, then I can spend some time with Fleur."

The taxi arrived and dropped Saron at the pub and John said he would give her a call. On the way to the Spinning Jenny John got a call from Lisa Tink.

"Hi John, sorry to bother you, but just came up to see how your sister was doing. The front door was wide open and there is no sign of her. I am a bit concerned."

"Listen Lisa, I am just picking my car up at the Spinning Jenny and I will be down see to you in fifteen minutes or so."

John was concerned as he got the car and drove to Cambridge Lodge. Lisa was waiting outside when he arrived.

"Still no sign, Lisa?"

"No John, I wonder if she has gone walking and forgot the door."

"Possibly, I best have a look round."

All Fleur's clothes were still hung up, but he did notice a blood stain in the kitchen. Lisa hadn't spotted it, so he wiped it up and put it in an evidence bag.

BODY PARTS

"I have tried to ring her, Lisa. I have locked the door and I will keep trying her. There will be a perfectly good explanation. I will call you later, Lisa."

Lisa looked worried but agreed with John. John kept trying Fleur for most of the day, but her phone was switched off. It was 6.00pm when his phone lit up and it was a message from Fleur.

'Get my things out of the lodge John. I will explain next time I see you. Love Fleur.'

John tried to ring the number, but it was dead again. John rang Lisa.

"Hi Lisa, panic over. Fleur has been rushed back to Paris on urgent business, so she asked me to get her things together and pay the bill. She said to say how wonderful Cambridge Lodge is and she is sorry. I'm afraid Fleur can be a bit dippy at times, Lisa."

"Not a problem John, as long as she is ok."

John arrived at Cambridge Lodge and collected all Fleur's things. He wanted to pay Lisa for the week, but she wouldn't let him.

"No John, just for the time she stayed please. I hope we will see her again."

John was thinking the same but couldn't say.

"Oh, I am sure of that, she loved the Lodge."

The next morning John see the point of being off for a couple of days now that Fleur had done one of her disappearing acts.

Gammon arrived at the Station.

BODY PARTS

"Morning Sir."

"Good morning Magic."

"DCI Dirk wants you to go straight to his office."

"Ok thanks."

John grabbed a coffee and headed into Dirk's office.

"Morning Sir."

"Morning John, take a seat. Brian Lund, I believe you had a lot to do with him back in the day, is that correct?"

"Yes, not my favourite person on the planet Sir."

"I thought so. I need to ask you where you were between the hours of 3.00am and 7.00am?"

"Why?"

"Mr Lund was found with his throat cut at his palatial house just outside Derby."

"What, and you think I murdered him?"

Series Three
Book Three
in the John Gammon Detective Series

"John, answer the question."

"Asleep at home, any further questions Sir?"

"Look John, the phone has been red hot from London. Brian Lund was an undercover informant for many years and this is a big loss."

"Maybe a big loss to you Sir, but I will celebrate the man's demise. He effectively killed my brother, my mother, my father and was instrumental in almost ruining my career so for me. It is a great day."

"John, I understand your feelings."

Gammon butted in, "That's just it, you don't understand my feelings. To imply that I have murdered a known criminal and to question my integrity as a serving police officer offends me. Now is that it Sir? I have work to do."

BODY PARTS

Dirk nodded, and Gammon left the office.

Gammon stood in a pensive mood looking out of his office window at Losehill. That's why his sister was over. She had come to kill Lund. She must have gone native on this one he thought. He just wished she would contact him. Then he remembered the blood he had on the handkerchief, so he nipped down to Wally. Gammon pulled Wally aside and explained.

"Just hoping this isn't Brian Lund's blood, Wally."

"Give me ten minutes John, and I will be able to tell you."

Gammon went back to his office and waited. Wally arrived true to his word.

"You are ok, John?"

"Whose is it?"

**Series Three
Book Three
in the John Gammon Detective Series**

"It's somebody called John Gammon of Bixton Police."

"What?"

"Roll your sleeves up."

"There was nothing on the left arm but a slight graze under the right arm.

"Well bloody hell Wally, thank goodness for that I never noticed it. Thanks mate."

Just as Wally was leaving Dirk was heading toward Gammon's office.

"Morning Wally," Dirk said as they passed outside Gammon's office.

Dirk went in.

"DI Gammon, you need to be aware that at 11.00am PSD will be here to talk to you."

"PSD?"

"Yes, Professional Standards Department and a MI5 agent."

BODY PARTS

"And what exactly do they want with me? We have a nutcase loose in the Peak District. He is chopping off people's arms and legs and they want to talk to me about a low-life scumbag, it's a bloody farce."

"I appreciate your feelings John, but I am only doing as I'm told. Make yourself available at 11.00am in interview room one."

Dirk slammed Gammon's door on his way out.

Gammon felt furious. Bloody Lund was even affecting his career from the grave. It was almost 10.52am when his phone flashed a message. It just said, 'Don't mention my name John, Fleur'.

Gammon immediately tried to ring the number, but it just said this number is unattainable.

Gammon knew they would probably want his phone, so he took out the SIM card. And smashed the phone before putting it in the skip outside. He taped the SIM card to the underside of his desk drawer.

He made his way to Interview room one. PSD and MI5 were already in the room. They stood up and gave John their cards.

"William Brown, senior investigating officer PSD. This is my colleague Gary Barry. Both Brown and Barry were big guys; over six foot three in their mid- fifties John thought.

"I am Lewis Dunn, MI5, DI Gammon."

Dunn was again mid–fifties with a grey moustache and slicked back grey hair.

"Detective Inspector Gammon, would you like a member of the Police Federation to be present?"

BODY PARTS

Gammon replied no.

"Ok. Your superior officer explained this morning that a former foe of yours, Mr Brian Lund, has been found dead with his throat cut."

"And your point is?"

Barry's lips curled in a cynical smile.

"Well from our point of view that puts you very much in the frame."

"Does it really Mr Barry?"

"Tell me DI Gammon, do you have any family; mother, father, brothers or sisters?"

Gammon knew this was a loaded question. It had all come clear to him why Fleur didn't want to stay with him.

"I am quite sure that you have the answer to that question and many more you intend asking me."

"Just answer the question, DI Gammon," Brown said in a firm tone.

"Ok, I have no family alive today; mother, father brother or sister."

"Are we sure about your answer, DI Gammon?"

"Yes, I am sure. Check with my solicitor who was left my parents will etc."

"We already have, DI Gammon. Why was the farm left by your father to a Mr Glazeback?"

"I don't know, you would have to ask my father that question."

"Did this annoy you?"

"Not in the slightest."

John was just hoping that they hadn't sussed out that he wasn't Philip's son but that his Uncle Graham was his biological father.

"DI Gammon, Brian Lund played a very important role for MI5 and we know you blamed him for your family's demise."

BODY PARTS

"I didn't just blame him. I hated him and to be honest the news this morning that a low-life scumbag like Brian Lund had been supposedly murdered filled me with hope for the future of mankind."

"Let me tell you about Brian Lund, DI Gammon. Mr Lund was recruited by MI5 eighteen years ago. Yes, I agree with you he wasn't a nice man, and to some degree he had politicians and the like in his pocket. But what he never had was MI5 bowing to his every mood swing. We were only interested in the information he could give us. How he came about the information was of no concern to us. We have investigated the scene and it was carried out very professionally. There are no clues. This could have been carried out by a serving police officer, or it could have been by a rogue undercover serving agent, or even somebody close to him that needed him silencing. Whoever it was we will find them. You are not the only suspect."

Gammon laughed, "So I am a suspect? Really?"

"Whilst we have interviewed you we have also been doing a thorough search of your home, DI Gammon."

"What? You have no right."

"I think you will find we do, if I consider the death of Mr Lund could affect national security, DI Gammon."

"You talk shit, Dunn."

"It is clear to all around this table that you have an uncontrollable temper Gammon, which is one of the reasons you are a suspect."

"Well gentlemen, depending on what we find at DI Gammon's home may depend on if we speak with him again. Good day," and Lewis Dunn stood up and left the room.

This left Barry and Brown who then also got up. Brown had the final word.

"If we find you have had any involvement, even the slightest, in the demise of Brian Lund your career will be over. So be very careful from now Gammon," and they left.

Gammon was seething. He went straight to his office grabbed his coat and told PC Magic on the desk he was leaving for the day. He had got the SIM card so he needed a phone urgently. John headed for the local mobile shop in Bixton and bought himself a new phone. Then he headed home.

Just as he arrived Phyllis Swan was leaving. She stopped her car.

"Hello John, those horrible men have just left, so I tided up after them."

"Sorry about that, Phyllis."

"No worries John. Oh, and these are yours."

Luckily for John she had taken the letters that Fleur had written over the past months.

"What made you remove these Phyliss?"

"I overheard them at the door when I was upstairs cleaning. They said they had to prove you had a sister or brother alive, that maybe was in, I think they said MI6. I wasn't sure, so I ran downstairs grabbed the letters from your half-sister and put them in my coat pocket."

"Did they ask you if I had a sister or brother?"

"Yes they did, but I told them you had no living relative, Mr Gammon."

"Thanks Phyllis, I have done nothing wrong, but they are looking to blame somebody for the murder of a very nasty man. A man I despised so they think I had involvement and I didn't."

John felt like kissing Phyllis because that was a close shave. Now more relieved he headed to the only person he knew he could talk to, Kev at the Spinning Jenny.

Kev was in his usual place behind the bar, sitting at one end reading the Racing Post.

"You looking to buy a race horse for your retirement, Kev?"

"Hey John, no mate. A bit out of my league but will be going to plenty of meetings."

"Don't blame the both of you mate, you have worked hard and deserve your retirement."

"You are early tonight lad, something on your mind?"

"Here, let me buy you a Pedigree and we can have a chat. I can't see many being in before 6.00pm, then Tracey Rodgers is coming in to do a shift for me."

Kev got the Pedigree they sat down.

"Is it Saron again?"

"No mate, so far so good on that front."

"Your Fleur is the spitting image of you and what a lovely girl."

"Thanks Kev."

"So, what's the problem, and where is she tonight? I thought you would have been spending some time with her while she is over."

"That's just it Kev. I had planned to have today and tomorrow off with her, but she has disappeared again."

"What do you mean disappeared?"

"Look Kev, what I tell you, you must take to your grave."

BODY PARTS

"Bloody hell that's harsh lad."

"Fleur works on the dark side of policing and the Secret Service. You remember how upset I was that Brian Lund wasn't dead. I was annoyed with Fleur when she told me, and I intended to speak to her about it."

"Ok so what?"

"Well, Lund was killed, he had his throat cut."

"So, what's the problem? I'm not following."

"Well MI6 and two officers from PSD."

"What's PSD?"

"It's a Professional Standards Department basically Internal Affairs. You see Lund was protected. He was a grass and quite high up apparently. That's why he got away with what he did over the years. Anyway because of our history they questioned me in depth. I never mentioned

Fleur because she always said I mustn't. She wouldn't stop at mine, she said she couldn't, so she stopped at Lisa and Jim Tink's place Cambridge Lodge. It all started falling into place. I think she killed Lund for me Kev."

"Blimey, you sure you haven't been watching too many films, John lad?"

"No mate, this is real."

"Well my advice to you is carry on as normal, because she has done you and Derbyshire a favour, if you are correct."

"If who's correct?"

"Oh nothing, Doreen. John was just saying Wednesday might make the play offs for us if they win their game in hand and Millwall lose theirs."

"Hope you are right John. It was lovely to see you and Saron together. Fleur was a

pretty girl that was talking to her most of
the night."

Kev thought quick.

"Have you done sandwiches for the darts
team tonight?"

"Bloody hell John, he is always thinking
of his stomach."

"Of course I have, you lummock!"

Doreen disappeared back to the kitchen.

"Phew, that was close Kev."

"You bet."

"Get me another pint mate and what are
you having? Are the rumours right about
Carol Lestar and Jimmy Lowcee buying the
place?

"Jimmy has approached us, but he wants
a lease and I think we would prefer a sale.
If he got it he said he would make Carol
Lestar bar manager, but we will see."

"Well Carol's well liked Kev, and it wouldn't seem like a massive change to folk."

"You are probably right, but let's wait and see, it's early days yet."

By 9.00pm Tracey was behind the bar and the pub was packed. Kev was throwing darts and playing dominoes for the Spinning Jenny, so John called it a night.

Back at his cottage his new book had arrived from Amazon. It was called Grove, the last part of a trilogy he had been reading. He sat down looking out of the back of the house with a large Jameson's and his book.

It was 3.00am when John suddenly woke feeling a bit cold.

He had fallen asleep, so he put his glass in the sink and made his way to bed.

BODY PARTS

The following morning John took the scenic route to Bixton and stopped off at Beryl's butties. To his surprise DI Smarty and DI Lee were in there stuffing their faces with two of the biggest bacon butty doorstep sandwiches he had ever seen.

"Caught you both."

"Hiya John, tell you what we can't stop coming here since you told us about it mate."

Yeah, always been top food here lads."

"What was all that about yesterday? It looked serious."

Gammon laughed, "Serious for Brian Lund, he was found with his throat cut."

"Really John, well that's great news. Do they think you were involved?"

"Ye, but to be fair, I guess that is a likely assumption knowing my history and what the guy did to my family. Well here I am paying for your food mates, and we can celebrate. He was a bloody nasty piece of work. Live by the sword, die by the sword, so he got what was coming."

"Right, you two we best get to work, or Dirk will be on my case. I'm not his favourite person at the minute."

Smarty and Lee laughed.

"When have you been with any of the clown DCI's that have worked at Bixton?"

When they arrived at Bixton PC Magic stopped them at the front desk.

"DCI Dirk's wife must have rung six times. He didn't go home last night, and she is worried. I don't know what to say, Sir."

"Ok, Me and Smarty will pop over to their house and have a chat. He is probably on a course and not mentioned it."

BODY PARTS

"I have tried his mobile Sir, but it's switched off."

"Ok well, if turns up here call me."

"Come on Dave, let's go and see how the other live."

Smarty and Gammon headed to Ostrich House in Hittington, the home of DCI Dirk. The place was quite grand with a small drive to the front the house. It had been renovated by the previous owners from what had been a hospital in the second world war. It fell into disrepair and was now quite grand. Gammon rang the doorbell and Dirk's wife came to the door. Sarah Dirk was a well-dressed woman in her late forties with strawberry coloured hair. She would have been possibly five feet nine John thought.

"Mrs Dirk?" DI Gammon and Smarty and he showed her their warrant cards.

"We believe you are concerned about DCI Dirk?"

"Yes DI Gammon, Saul came home about 5.45pm last night. He always plays squash at the squash club on a Tuesday, then has his dinner when he returns about 8.30pm but he never showed up."

"Ok well, I am sure there is a perfectly normal explanation."

"The squash club, where is it?"

"It's at Minky Mill in Ackbourne. It was converted some years ago by Albert Minky, a builder. It's very popular apparently."

"Did DCI Dirk play with the same person every week?"

"I think there were three guys, so Saul made up the four."

"Have you got their names and maybe addresses?"

"Sorry, I only know their names. Sebastian Stanley, James Zirckle and Lewis James."

"Ok, well look Mrs Dirk, we will pop over to the squash club and see what we can find out. Rest assured we will find DCI Dirk."

"Thank you, DI Gammon and DI Smarty," and she shook their hands.

"Some place they have here John, on a DCI's money."

"Yeah, but don't think they have any children and I think Mrs Dirk's family own a meat packing company."

They arrived at the converted Minky Mill and went straight to reception. It was a nice set up and the young girl on reception was very pleasant. They showed their warrant cards and asked if Mr Dirk had been in last night.

"Just a moment, we have an electric scanner. Anybody that comes through that door is scanned and if they are a member the screen will show it then register it on this sheet. No, it doesn't appear to have scanned Mr Dirk."

"Do you have the addresses of these gentlemen please?"

Gammon showed her the names Mrs Dirk gave him.

"Were they here last night?"

"No, I know they wouldn't have been. They are on a golfing holiday in Portugal with Mr Minky, but I will double check for you."

After a few minutes she stated that they weren't there last night.

"Thank you very much for all your help," and they left.

"So where was he John?"

BODY PARTS

"My gut feeling is he is having an affair."

"Really?"

"It has all the hallmarks to me, Dave."

On the way back to Bixton PC Magic called Gammon's mobile.

Gammon answered, "Yes Magic, how can I help you?"

"Sir, I have some bad news. DCI Dirk has been found by a golfer on the golf course in Micklock. He has been disfigured."

"What?"

"John Walvin and forensics are at the scene. He said to tell you his right arm has been removed and he bled to death."

"Ok, myself and DI Smarty will go straight to Micklock Golf Course."

Gammon sped to Micklock and parked at the golf course. The same jobs-worthy from last time he was there came running out.

"You can't park there, this is a member's only car park."

Gammon couldn't be doing with him. He locked the car, showed his warrant card and him and Smarty strode off down the fairway to where forensics were. Gammon put his head in the tent.

"Get out John, you are contaminating the scene."

Wally came out.

"Not good John. Poor DCI Dirk had his right arm removed from the shoulder and was left to bleed to death. My guess is he wasn't killed here. Like the others who were dumped when they were so weak from loss of blood."

BODY PARTS

"Need everything on this for a 9.00am meeting with everyone, Wally."

"Understand, John."

"Come on Dave, we best go back and give Mrs Dirk the bad news."

They arrived back at Ostrich house just as Mrs Dirk was getting in her car.

"Oh, that was quick, Mr Gammon. Has he turned up at work?"

"Can we come inside, Mrs Dirk."

"Of course, would you like a drink?"

"Please sit down, Mrs Dirk. I am afraid DCI Dirk was found murdered by a golfer. His body had been left at Micklock Golf Club."

Dirk's wife screamed.

"Get Mrs Dirk some water, Dave."

"Have you got anybody that can sit with you?"

"No, we had no children and all my family are no longer with us," she said, shaking and crying in equal measures.

"Would you like me to get a bereavement councillor over here?"

"No, I will be fine. It's just me and Saul have been together since school, he was my only boyfriend. We were devastated when we could not have children. But we had each other, and now I have lost the only thing I love," and she cried some more.

"I think it would be best if I got DI Scooper over to sit with you."

She nodded in agreement.

"I like Sandra, she is a nice girl DI Gammon."

"Please call me John."

She smiled at him.

BODY PARTS

Within the hour Scooper had arrived and Gammon said, "Stay as long as Mrs Dirk needs you, please Sandra."

CHAPTER FOUR

Gammon and Smarty left.

"What was the name of the two PCs taking that gentleman's details who found Dirk?"

"PC Crunch and PC Beglin, apparently very good officers, John."

"Ok, let Magic know I need them in the meeting in the morning please Dave. I am assuming Sandra will accompany Mrs Dirk to formally identify DCI Dirk's body."

"Yes, she said she would as we left, John."

They drove back to Bixton both quite shocked that a colleague had been a victim of the killer. Once back at Bixton Gammon started opening his post and there was a letter from the killer.

BODY PARTS

'Dear John

Could not believe my luck when the guy in the squash gear had stopped to fix his tyre and there is me looking for an arm. I offered to help him then bludgeoned him with the wheel brace. It wasn't until I stripped him and removed his arm that his warrant card fell out of his track suit pocket only a DCI at Bixton. If you get promotion will you let me off?' and he ended with a row of smiley faces.

'Speak soon John'

That was it. Gammon felt physically sick. He had only yesterday had a bit of a run in with Dirk, but overall they had got on ok

Gammon put the letter in a clear evidence bag, not that he was expecting Wally to find anything, but that was Police procedure. Gammon left it with the only person in forensics and said to give it to Wally. Now he had to contact the head of Derbyshire Police, Chicf Constable Andrew Sim.

"Could I speak with Chief Constable Sim, I am Detective Inspector Gammon of Bixton Police."

"Just a moment," the voice said. Eventually Andrew Sim answered.

"Chief Constable Andrew Sim, how may I help you?"

Gammon cleared his throat and told Sim what had happened. Sim was clearly shocked and said he would be at Bixton at 10.00am to see Gammon. Gammon decided he best make his office look tidy, so he cleared all the papers and tidied round.

BODY PARTS

The following morning they held the meeting in the incident room. Gammon stood up.

"Ok everybody, I am sure you are all aware that we lost DCI Dirk to the killer who is stalking the Peak District. DCI Dirk was one of us and we owe his wife to ensure we leave no stone unturned in finding his killer."

"I just want to run through what we have so far in this case, which to be honest is very little."

"Victim one was Alan Hewitt, a body builder and security guard at local clubs, his left arm was severed.

Victim two, Larry Bailey, found with both his legs removed.

Victim three, DCI Dirk, found with his right arm severed."

"We currently only have one suspect, a Peter Scarthin, but to be honest I don't really think he is credible."

"So, anybody got any ideas to take this forward?"

"Yes Scooper."

"I know this sounds obvious, but he appears to be collecting body parts. Is he using them as specimens?"

"Can I hold you there Sandra? Why do you think it's a man?"

"Just where the bodies were found. They were quite big men."

"It could be two men, it could be two women or a woman working alone or a man working alone."

Sandra sat back down a bit annoyed at John's put down.

"Yes, DI Lee."

BODY PARTS

"I remember a case in the late forties. I read about where this guy was collecting body parts and putting them in formaldehyde to preserve them. He was going to experiment with them."

"I read that also," said DI Milton. "Didn't they nickname him The Doctor?"

Wally stood up.

"A body can be preserved in formaldehyde and a chemical asmethanol, which is basically embalming fluid injected into the body."

"Ok thanks Wally."

"DI Scooper, do some research on our only suspect Peter Scarthin; usual stuff, bank accounts, where he has worked in the last twenty years, if he knew any of the victims."

"DI Milton, I want you to look at any connections with the people that found the bodies. Also check if DCI Dirk had at any time arrested any of the victims and Scarthin."

"Finally everyone, I have Chicf Constable Andrew Sim of Derbyshire police here to speak to me at 10.00am, so best behaviour everyone."

"Oh, and DI Lee, no morning Cornish pasties strewn across your desk please."

Everyone laughed.

"Thanks everyone, give me a report in the morning please Sandra and Carl on your findings."

They left the meeting and Gammon told Magic that as soon as Sim arrived he was to show him to his office and offer him a drink. He was also to use the china cups not plastic ones.

Andrew Sim arrived at John's office with PC Magic doing his impression of an

BODY PARTS

Upstairs Downstairs butler. Chief Constable sat down in the chair opposite Gammon.

"Nice view you have, DI Gammon."

"Yes, I like it Sir."

"Well I will cut straight to the chase. I was Chief Constable in Norfolk until six months ago when I was transferred to Derbyshire. I've been very lucky John, we love the area. I believe you were born near here, is that correct?"

"Yes, my parents had a farm near Hittington, so I grew up in the area."

"Well I also hear that you were a high-flying officer in London."

"Not sure about high flying, Sir."

"You don't have to be modest with me, John. I have read your file. Tell me, you turned down a special job in the force, why was that?"

Series Three
Book Three
in the John Gammon Detective Series

"I didn't think my work was finished here, Sir. At the time I was engaged, and my partner didn't want to move."

"So, are you married, John?"

"No Sir, another long story in the life of John Gammon I'm afraid."

"I do believe you have to find a really good women who can understand the pressure our jobs bring. I am afraid they are few and far between."

Gammon quite liked this guy he seemed down to earth and somebody he thought he could work with.

"It's very sad about DI Dirk, John. I have to say at this point he wasn't my choice, and I like to have people working for me with the same attention to detail. Which brings me to my next question. How would you like to take the position of DCI at Bixton, John?"

BODY PARTS

Gammon wasn't expecting that was this his chance. He quite liked Chief Constable Sim.

"I don't know what to say, Sir."

"I have no concern that you can't do this job, John. The amount of DCIs this station has gone through tells me you run it anyway."

"In that case, I want to accept Sir."

"Great John, you will need a replacement for yourself on the team. Although I know you will be a hands-on DCI like I was, it's in you. Let me know if you have anybody you wish to promote, or failing that we can put our heads together and come up with somebody."

"Now DCI Gammon, first of all congratulations, but secondly I heard a sniff that the press boys will be circling, now that one of our own has been murdered. If you need my input day or night this is my personal number, John."

"Thank you, Sir."

"Right, I have a golfing tournament in aid of Derbyshire Cave rescue and I am teeing off first. I will give you a call later on in the week just to catch up."

Chief Constable Sim left. Gammon sat at his desk he could hardly contain his happiness.

He told PC Magic to get everybody together in interview room one as he had an announcement. Gammon left it five minutes then went down. The room was buzzing.

"You aren't leaving, are you John?"

"No Dave, the opposite. I just wanted to tell you all that as of now the Chief Constable of Derbyshire, Andrew Sim, has asked me to take the position of DCI here at Bixton, and I have accepted."

There was a thunderous round of applause. They all individually came up and shook his hand.

"Ok, I really appreciate your support everybody. Now let's get this killer caught and set me off on a good footing."

"Oh, my first thing is I would like the station to be represented at DCI Dirk's funeral; four DCIs, two Sergeants and a couple of PCs. If you can give me names please, as I would imagine Mrs Dirk will want the station to carry the coffin. Thanks again everybody."

It was now 4.45pm. Gammon sat in his office and called Saron with the good news. Donna answered.

"Hi John, how are you?"

"Very good thanks Donna. Is Saron about?"

"She has gone with her mum to Ireland for a week, did she not say?"

"Probably, but we did have a few Saturday night."

"Is there anything I can help you with?"

"No, just ringing Saron to tell I have been made up to DCI here at Bixton."

"Oh John, that's wonderful news. It should have happened years ago I might add, but better late than never. Really pleased for you John."

Gammon decided to call it a night and left. As he walked past PC Magic on the front desk Magic asked if he could have a word.

"Congratulations Sir."

"Thank you, Magic."

BODY PARTS

"I wondered if that might help me and my position."

"Bloody hell Magic, I can't work miracles. Well not yet anyway, but keep your nose clean, and maybe a year or so I'll see what I can do."

Magic looked crestfallen as Gammon left. He decided to nip and tell Kev his good news, he was still buzzing.

"Bloody hell lad, you look pleased with yourself. Have you won the lottery?"

"The equivalent for me, Kev. I have been made up to DCI at Bixton."

Suddenly a head popped up from behind the bar. Doreen had been cleaning the shelves.

"Come here," and she kissed John on the cheek.

**Series Three
Book Three
in the John Gammon Detective Series**

"Could not happen to a nicer lad. Now you have got what you wanted, get working on Saron and bloody settle down lad."

John just had a couple with Kev and Doreen made him bangers and mash to take out. He decided he was going to get his book finished. Little did he know what was waiting for him at his home.

It was 8.10pm when he arrived back feeling contented, with his favourite bangers and mash to consume. John opened the door put his dinner on the table and nipped to the downstairs toilet. He hadn't noticed the black bin liner on his table. Phyllis Swan would often make a point of picking up his clothes and putting them in a bin liner, so he didn't take much notice. He microwaved his dinner and sat and ate it. John picked up the bin liner and took it over to the washing machine. He did as he

BODY PARTS

always did and tipped the contents on the
floor. What rolled out almost made him
sick!

A head rolled under the chair and inside
the bag were two arms and two legs but no
torso. Gammon immediately phoned
Bixton station and said what had happened
and to get Wally's team over urgently. John
didn't touch anything but felt he needed a
change of clothes, so he went upstairs to
change before Wally arrived. On his
bedside table was a letter. He knew straight
away who it was from, so he opened it and
started to read.

'Dear John
It was with some regret that I broke into
your house and left you my day's work. The
man is Raitus Emsar. He is a Polish

immigrant and had a nice torso so that's why he was chosen.

It won't be too long before you get the chance to see my work, I am sure you will be impressed.

Again I do apologise for breaking in but seeing that a policeman lives there it was quite easy my friend.

Bye for now'.

The day was ruined. All the good news today, and this nut case has taken that away by breaking into my house and leaving me the remnants of some poor guy and letter of apology. How sick is this guy he thought?

John rang the station and asked Di Trimble to get forensics to his house. He said to tell Magic in the morning to arrange a meeting for everyone in the incident room at 11.00am. That way it would give Wally time to get something he hoped.

By 3.00am the body parts had been removed and Wally and his team had left. John lay in bed thinking about the case. What exactly was this nutcase collecting body parts for and why. He knew he had no choice but to call in a criminal profiler to help with the case.

The following morning at the station John scoured the Police database for a profiler. One name stood out, Margaret Bradbury. Gammon called the number. She was based in Dorset.

"Good morning, Margaret Bradbury, how can I help?"

"Oh, hello Margaret, this is DCI John Gammon of Bixton Police in Derbyshire, we have a situation up here that we could do with some special skills to help us with the problem."

"Ok DCI Gammon, this is my e-mail address. Just write down what the problem is, and I will get back to you as soon as possible."

"Appreciate that Margaret, I will do that now."

Gammon rang off and started to type about the letters, which he also scanned in as an attachment, and he wrote down about how the victims were found.

Within a few minutes of sending the e-mail his mobile rang. It was Margaret.

"DCI Gammon, this really intrigues me. I worked on a case not too dissimilar to this in New Zealand. I can come to Derbyshire tomorrow if it helps. Could you arrange accommodation for me?"

BODY PARTS

John said he would try and get her into Lisa and Jim's place, and he would text her to let her know.

Gammon rang Lisa Tink.

"Hello John, good to hear from you. Did you find what had happened to your sister?"

"Yes Lisa, she has got quite a pressured job mainly in France, so had to return. I had a missed text from her."

"It's not a problem John, as long as it was nothing to do with the accommodation."

"No, nothing like that, I mean the Lodge is fabulous. Which brings me to why I rang. I have a colleague from Dorset that may need a couple of weeks accommodation. Is the Lodge free?"

"Oh John, I am fully booked for the whole of the summer."

"Well I'm not surprised."

"I do have a room at the B and B. It's en suite and very nice. Eighty pounds a night for single occupancy and it's on the farm, but it's an apartment."

"Book me that please Lisa. The lady's name is Margaret Bradbury and you can invoice me at Bixton Police please?"

"Great John, what time will she arrive?"

"I would say mid-afternoon, is that ok?"

"Perfect John, don't worry she will be well looked after."

"Thanks Lisa, I will see you later with Margaret."

John called Margaret back and said he would meet her in the Spinning Jenny then take her to the B & B. She said she would be there about 4.00pm. Gammon let DI Smarty know what he was doing and carried on with his paperwork. By 11.00am everybody was assembled in the incident room.

Gammon stood at the front.

"Ok everybody, some time yesterday somebody broke into my house. Sadly, they left me a present of some body parts in a bin liner. On my bed side table they left a note which I gave to Wally."

John Walvin stood up.

"I am afraid the note had nothing that could lead us to anything or anybody. But under the finger nails of one of the severed arms we found flour. My long guess is the killer could be a chef or he works in a flour mill."

Smarty stood up.

"A chef makes sense, he would have the knives to do the work."

The murmurings in the room seemed to agree with Smarty.

Series Three
Book Three
in the John Gammon Detective Series

"No DNA, Wally."

"No, sorry John."

"Today I am bringing in a criminal profiler to help with the case. Her name is Margaret Bradbury, she is from Dorset and I would like you to give her your full support. We need the help. She will start tomorrow here at Bixton."

"Ok, Sandra and Carl have you got anything for us?"

DI Milton stood up.

"Right Sir. Peter Scarthin was arrested in 1987 on gun charges. He basically had fired a double barrel shotgun at what he said were gypsies trying to break into his outbuildings. The arresting officer was Sergeant Matkin who had done his Sergeant training with our very own DCI Saul Dirk. Although Dirk went on in his career, Sergeant Matkin never rose any higher. He was eventually thrown off the force after an altercation with Scarthin in the Wobbly Man pub in Toad Holes."

"Is Matkin still alive?"

"I checked that Sir. He is retired and lives in sheltered accommodation in Micklock."

"Ok thanks Carl."

"Sandra, have you found anything?"

"A couple of things, Sir. Scarthin was left Lavender farm by a Mrs Cosgrove. Mrs Cosgrove had two children; Larry Bailey our victim number two and John Glew who found the body. Both children she adopted. The first one she adopted when she was married to Hank Bailey, the second child she adopted as a baby when she was married to Martin Glew. Both men died, and she married Paul Cosgrove."

Series Three
Book Three
in the John Gammon Detective Series

"Wow, so John Glew was Larry Bailey's half-brother."

"DI Lee and Smarty, get John Glew in for questioning please."

"Ok thanks everybody. "

It was almost 1.00pm when Lee and Smarty arrived back with John Glew and Magic said he was in interview room one. Gammon headed down and Lee did the necessary introductions on tape. Glew had requested his lawyer to be present, a Mr Broome, a small bespectacled man from Goven and Wild solicitors in Bixton.

"Ok Mr Glew, thank you for coming. I am DCI Gammon this is DI Smarty and over there is DI Lee. Mr Glew, you found the body of Larry Bailey, is that correct?"

"Yes."

BODY PARTS

"Just refresh me why were you at Hittington Fishing Lake that day?"

"I am training for the Derby Marathon."

"Yes, I believe looking at your notes that's what you told my officers. What you didn't tell my officers was Larry Bailey was your step brother."

"Why DCI Gammon, would I want to admit to that lump of lard being any relation to me, which he isn't."

"So, are you telling me that you and Larry didn't get on?"

"I was a baby when he was seven and he always disliked me, because his nose got pushed out. So, for what it's worth, I had no feelings when I found his body. If that makes me a suspect, then the system is wrong, Mr Gammon."

"I do feel there seems to be a lot of hatred for your step brother, way beyond a general dislike shall we say. Tell me Mr Glew is there something you are not telling me?"

Glew looked at his solicitor who gestured with his eyes to tell Glew to speak.

"When I was first married I had been away working in Scotland and my wife Andrea was at home. She worked at the toy factory in Dilley Dale as a quality engineer. You are probably aware that Larry also worked there. Anyway, he was always jealous of me and one night whilst I was away, the girls from the toy factory arranged a mixed pool night for some charity. Andrea got a little bit the worse for wear and Larry said he would make sure she got home ok. Nobody knew of our dislike for each-other, so everyone just thought he was being kind."

BODY PARTS

"To cut a long story short."

At this point Glew reached for his glass of water clearly feeling uncomfortable telling the story. Glew continued.

"He took Andrea home and to the day she died she said he had drugged her drink, but she could remember him forcing himself on her, but it wasn't clear."

"I tackled Bailey about it and we had a massive row, but June his wife said he had just dropped Andrea off. He was back in the house by 11.10pm. When I checked the time they left with the taxi driver, he said he dropped Bailey and my wife off at our home at 10.30pm. Bailey said he walked home after making sure Andrea was in the house, and it was thirty minutes to his house. I had to let it go at that because he would not have had time to do what Andrea said he did."

"Where is your wife now?"

"Andrea died when she was having our son Toby."

"Did Toby ever know the story?"

"No, I'm afraid me and Toby don't get on. I loved Andrea and I think I subconsciously blamed him for Andrea's death."

"So, you are telling me that Toby knew nothing of the feud between you and your step brother."

"No, and to be honest, because we had different names, to this day he doesn't know of mine and Larry Bailey's association. I never saw Bailey again or spoke to him after the incident with Andrea."

"Ok Mr Glew, you are free to go but we may need to question you further."

Glew and his solicitor left.

BODY PARTS

"That's some story, Sir."

"I agree, Peter. What do you think, Dave?"

"It seems to me that Glew carries a grudge and I guess you can't blame him."

"Are you two thinking what I am thinking?"

"What about Toby Glew?"

"Yes. I think there is a chance that Toby is Larry's son, and I think Glew knew that. Hence the poor relationship with Toby."

"Shall we get Toby in for questioning?"

"No, not yet. Let's see how this pans out, but there is more to John Glew than I first thought, gentlemen."

Gammon went back to his office and worked on some new paperwork he had to fill in now he was DCI of Bixton.

Series Three
Book Three
in the John Gammon Detective Series

Gammon suddenly realised the time it was 3.50pm and he was meeting Margaret Bradbury at 4.00pm at the Spinning Jenny.

John arrived at 4.15pm and rushed down the steps to the bar. Kev was at the end of the bar talking to a slim blonde. Nobody else was in the pub so John thought it must be Margaret Bradbury.

"He's here, look you. How could you be late for such a startling woman? John Gammon hang your head in shame," and Kev laughed as he poured John a pint.

John walked up to the lady.

"I am assuming you must be Margaret Bradbury?"

"The very one, so you must be DCI John Gammon?"

"Yes, pleased to meet you, Margaret."

Margaret Bradbury was in her early forties and quite tall with shoulder length blonde hair and a really pretty face. She reminded John of Debbie Harry with her facial bone structure. Margaret Bradbury was dressed in a plain blue business suit with a cream open neck shirt.

"I have heard a lot about you, DCI Gammon."

"Please call me John."

"Then you must call me Marg or Margaret, but please never Maggie," and she laughed.

"Why not Maggie?"

"Oh, it a New Zealand thing. I was out there working for New Zealand police for four years and they shorten everybody's name. I got to the point where I hated flippin' Maggie, John and still do."

John could see this was going to be one formidable lady on his team. They had two drinks and John offered Margaret something to eat. But she said she had some work to catch up and she had picked up a sandwich on the way up. They left the Spinning Jenny and drove the short distance to the next village of Clough Dale and Lisa and Jim Tink's B and B.

Lisa was waiting to greet Margaret. She did this with all her guests and made them feel at home.

"Look Margaret, I will pick you up at 8.30am if that's ok. I can show you the route to Bixton then after that you will be fine."

"Ok, thanks John, this place is fabulous."

Margaret was enthusing as Lisa showed her round. John left them to it and headed for the Spinning Jenny. Just before he landed in the car park his phone rang. It was DI Smarty.

"Sir, we have a concern."

BODY PARTS

"What's the problem, Dave?"

"DI Scooper's mum just rang the station. Sandra was supposed to pick her daughter up from a friend's house in Cramford, but she never arrived. Her friend phoned Sandra's mum, but she had heard nothing, so she phoned work to see if she was delayed. DI Scooper left just after 5.00pm, Sir."

"Maybe she has broken down on the way, have you phoned her mobile?"

"Yes, and it's dead, Sir."

"Ok Dave. Where in Cramford was she heading? Let's go and pick Rosie up. I will meet you there, then let's follow her route back to Bixton."

Gammon set off for the address Smarty had given him; The Olde Blacksmith Shop in Cramford.

Gammon was the first there, so he showed his warrant card and spoke with Lydia Duster whose child Rosie had gone to play with.

"This isn't like Sandra, Mr Gammon."

"I am sure there will be a perfectly good explanation, Mrs Duster."

"Just then DI Smarty arrived.

"Dave, you take Rosie to Pritwich and hand her over to Sandra's mum. I will trace her route back to Bixton in case she has broken down."

Gammon thanked Mrs Duster and set of back to Bixton. The weather had turned, and it was howling it down like only the Peak District weather could if it so wished.

John's windscreen wipers were hardly keeping up as he came down towards Alford in the Water, a pretty little village with a small stone humped coaching bridge. He spotted what he thought was Sandra's British racing green Mercedes CLK. She had only had the car three weeks and was always giving Gammon stick about her motor being superior to his.

Gammon pulled over but there was no sign of Sandra. John tried the door and it opened. There was blood on the inside of the door. Gammon immediately phoned Wally, Smarty and DI Lee to get over there. It was now no longer a case of she was late, it was now a crime scene.

Gammon sat in his car and waited. The weather was just getting worse Wally was the first to arrive with three of his staff. They set up the obligatory white tent round Sandra's car.

"Sir, look this is Sandra's shoe."

Smarty handed John Sandra's shoe absolutely covered in mud.

"There are some tracks as well, here look. It appears to me that she has been dragged to this clearing."

Gammon, Smarty and Lee headed towards the clearing full of apprehension. Sandra's other shoes was sitting in a puddle of rainwater.

"She has been abducted, Sir."

"But why?" John asked. "I don't understand, Dave. What do you think, Peter?"

"I'm with DI Smarty. It clearly looks like she has been abducted and put up a hell of a fight."

Gammon called the station and told Magic he wanted as many constables and dogs as possible to the scene urgently. The realisation was kicking in. Sandra had been taken and he was sure of that. By now DI Milton had arrived.

BODY PARTS

"Carl, go to Sandra's mother's house in Pritwich and carefully break it to her that we think she may have been abducted."

"Ok Sir."

Police were all over the scene with sniffer dogs, but the trail appeared cold.

"There isn't anything more we can do here lads. Call it a night and we will have to see if whoever has Sandra contacts us."

Before he left he told everyone to be in the incident room at 9.00am prompt and he asked Wally for something, anything that might help find Sandra.

John couldn't face the pub and went straight home. He and Sandra had been lovers and workmates and his stomach was churning as he opened his cottage door. Nailed to the stair bannister was a photo. It was Sandra covered in mud. Her face was cut and she looked dreadful. John removed the picture. On the back the abductor had written.

'Another one to my collection soon you will know John Gammon'

Gammon called Wally who he could hardly hear with the rain lashing down on the incident tent. Wally said he didn't expect there would be any trace of the person on the photograph, but to bring it in the morning.

John climbed the stairs. Yet again whoever was committing these crimes seemed able to break into John's house whenever he wanted, and he knew he had to do something about that.

The following morning on the way to pick up Margaret from Lisa's bed and breakfast he called police security and asked for cameras to be discreetly fitted that he could monitor on his phone and laptop. He told them he had left a key under the bird table in the back garden.

John arrived, and Margaret was outside waiting. She looked even more stunning that when he picked her up the day before. The weather had altered dramatically, and it was quite a nice day.

"Morning John."

"Morning Margaret, everything ok?"

"It is fabulous John, and what a lovely couple Jim and Lisa are. They took me to a pub called the Wobbly Man in a little village called Toad Holes, and they insisted on buying me a meal. Don't think I have ever come across such a lovely set up."

On the way to Bixton John explained about DI Scooper.

"She is a real valued member of our team and my concern is this serial killer who is dismembering his victim will do the same to Sandra."

"Understand your concern. As soon as I get set up I will get started on profiling this person or persons. I am assuming there is a lot of collated information so far, John?"

"Yes, we have a lot which I will give you. Also you have full access to John Walvin's department. He is head of forensics."

"Ok, that's great."

Gammon and Bradbury arrived at Bixton and Bradbury certainly got some looks from Smarty and Milton who were talking to Magic at the front desk.

Gammon showed Margaret to what was DCI Dirk's office. Gammon didn't want to move into that office, he loved the view he had of Losehill from his office window.

BODY PARTS

"Right Margaret, that's the wifi code, here are some case files," and Gammon dumped four thick folders of paperwork.

"The coffee machine is at the end of the corridor and I am next door but one. I will show you to the incident room at 9.00am for me to introduce you to the team."

"Ok, thanks John."

Gammon left her office and grabbed a cup of coffee, why he didn't know, it was just habit. The coffee would not have been out of place in a muddy river.

With the team assembled Gammon brought Margaret Bradbury into the room to be introduced. He also had news on Magic's replacement to announce.

"Ok everybody, I would like to introduce Margaret Bradbury. She will be staying in the Peak District until the person, or persons, are identified that we are investigating for the serial murders of the victims with dismembered bodies. Remember Margaret is here to help us, so please whatever she asks for from the team ensure we support her. Over to you Margaret."

"Thank you, DCI Gammon. Just to give you some background, I am a criminal profiler with forensic psychology experience. I have worked with numerous police forces in the UK and Ireland as well as MI5 and MI6."

"For me to help you catch whoever is responsible you need some guidelines, and I need lots of information to achieve a judgement that could possibly lead to an arrest."

"My most famous case was in New Zealand, when my profiling allowed the New Zealand police to apprehend a woman

who for five years had eluded them. I am
sure you will have heard of her. Her name
was Maria Vasquez. She had poisoned over
forty people and possibly more. She was a
trained vet and her killing spree began
because she was sacked from her position
with Woola Bunga Nature Reserve, just
outside Brighton in the South Island. So,
my experience will help this case as long as
we work as a team."

"Thank you, Margaret. Now we get on to
one of our own."

Gammon showed the picture he had of
Sandra from the abductee. There was a
gasp and then silence in the room.

"We will find her, she is one of us."

"Next week we have a new DI starting,
Kate Bass. She is originally from the area
but moved to work in Cambridge. With her
knowledge of the area we should have a

good DI. I know you all feel Magic was a bit harshly treated by my predecessor, but there is little I could do about that as the ball was already rolling on this appointment."

"Ok everybody back to work, and let's hope Margaret comes up with the goods."

"Bloody hell, Dave," Carl Milton said to Smarty. "She is a looker and I didn't see a ring on her finger."

"No, I didn't but agree mate that is one tasty woman."

"I think I like working here, Dave," and Milton laughed as he left the room.

BODY PARTS

CHAPTER FIVE

Three weeks passed with no more word from the serial killer and no joy in finding Sandra Scooper. Gammon was sitting with Margaret Bradbury. She said she had collected something together.

"Go on then Margaret, because boy do we need some help."

"Well I believe our killer is male. He works alone and doesn't like women. I would say he has had troubled relationships, that possibly being the reason for his dislike of women. He is not your archetypal loner, in fact I would say this guy has friends, and maybe in some kind of club."

"The body parts are most possibly trophies of some kind. That bit I am not sure of. I believe he is a local man possibly in his late forties. Is that enough to go on, John?"

"Well I think we should look into the background of John Glew and Toby Glew Margaret, because at the moment we have nothing else. Thanks Margaret, I will get the ball rolling."

Gammon called DI Milton and DI Smarty into the office.

"Right, that's the profile we know about John Glew. The age profile isn't far out, and he is a member of a running club. Let's get him in and Toby Glew. Let's shake the tree and see what falls out. Tell them they have the right to a solicitor, lads."

Smarty and Milton set off on their task and Gammon stood staring out at Losehill. It was raining again, and the droplets were running down the picture window, as if they were racing each other to a finish line.

BODY PARTS

Gammon had tried not to think too much about Sandra. He knew it would upset him. They had so much history together, it hardly seemed possible that she may not be alive, and not something John wanted to contemplate.

Smart and Milton arrived back almost together and put the Glews in separate interview rooms; John in one and Toby in two. John had a solicitor, but Toby declined one. Gammon decided to interview Toby first.

"Mr Glew, I am DCI John Gammon. This is my colleague DI Milton and DI Lee will record the interview."

Gammon gestured to DI Lee and he did the usual spiel, then pressed record.

"Mr Glew, may I call you Toby?"

Toby nodded. Toby Glew was about twenty three years old. Not quite to the profile but quite a muscular man who clearly worked out.

"So Toby, you don't wish to have a solicitor present, is that correct?"

"Yes."

"Ok Toby, you are the son of Andrea Glew and John Glew?"

This seemed to spook Toby.

"Yes, my mother was Andrea Glew."

"We are led to believe you and your father don't speak, or should I say get on, is that correct?"

"If you are referring to John Glew, then that is correct. He is a stuck-up arse hole."

"No love lost there then Toby. Why is that?"

"I think you should ask him."

"But I am asking you Toby."

"No comment."

BODY PARTS

"Come on Toby, help us out here. I know fathers and sons fall out Toby, but this seems like hatred to me."

"Good detective work there, Mr Gammon."

"Ok, so tell me a bit about you. Are you a member of a gym? You look like you work out."

"Yes, I am member at Muscles in Cramford."

"So, did you know Alan Hewitt?"

"Yes of course, Mr Steroid."

"I am guessing from that inference you weren't a fan."

"Not sure anybody at the club was, Mr Gammon."

This was interesting to Gammon, he had an association here.

"So why do you think Mr Hewitt was murdered?"

"Because like John Glew, he was an arse."

"So, are you a member of any other clubs or societies?"

"Yes, the Civil War Re-enactment Society from Winksworth, been a member for four years."

"What do you do for a living, Toby?"

"Meat Warehouse Supervisor."

"Where is that at?"

"Ackbourne, the company is Sterling's Wholesale Meat."

"So, what does your job entail?"

"Well now a lot of paperwork since I have been a Supervisor."

"Before that Toby?"

"I worked on the line cutting meat into joints and sometimes I could be on the wrapping machines."

BODY PARTS

"Did my officer pick you up from your home?"

Di Milton stepped in.

"No Sir, we went to the address we have for Toby, but his neighbour said he had moved. He worked at Sterling's meat warehouse in Ackbourne, so we picked him up there."

"Ok so Toby, where are you living currently?"

"I live at Cedric Fletcher's farm. He lets me stay there and I do jobs round the farm. I worked there as a kid. His daughter got in touch because her dad was going blind and struggled with the farm. He is eighty one years old, so she said I could live there rent free if I helped out. It was too good a deal to miss so I said yes."

"Cedric Fletcher's farm, where is that?"

"Between Dilley Dale and Rowksly."

"Ok Toby, well thanks for a frank and honest interview. We may need to speak again but other than that you are free to go."

Toby left and Milton turned off the tape.

"Well lads, what do you reckon?"

"He seems like a decent lad, Sir."

"What about the butcher job?"

"I think that is just a coincidence, my money is on his father, if indeed it is his father."

"Ok, let's go and see him now."

Glew was sitting with his solicitor, Mr Broome. Milton did the necessary introduction before setting the tape running. Broome straight away asked why his client was being interviewed again.

"This is tantamount to harassment, DCI Gammon. My client came in last time, answered all your questions, and yet here we are again doing the same thing. I would like this meeting to understand this is not being fair to my client."

"Have you quite finished, Mr Broome?"

Broome looked at Gammon in a stern way over the top of his glasses.

"Ok Mr Glew, we have just had a long chat with your son Toby. There is certainly no love lost from his side, in fact he quite dislikes you."

"What's your point, Mr Gammon?"

"I will come to that in a minute. Have you ever visited Alford in the Water Mr Glew?"

Glew put his hand to his mouth and spoke into Broome's ear.

Glew then replied, "Yes."

"Do you know Detective Inspector Sandra Scooper."

"Yes, I did."

"You said did, Mr Glew. Why would you use the past tense I wonder?"

"Well, it's all over the news that she is missing."

"What so you presume she is dead then?"

Glew became a bit flustered.

"Sorry, it was the wrong turn of phrase."

"How do you know Sandra Scooper?"

"Is this what this is about? You think I had something to do with the disappearance of Sandra Scooper."

"Answer the question, Mr Glew."

"I have known Sandra since she was a young girl. I am quite a keen gardener, and Lord and Lady Hasford at the manor house in Pritwich employed me at weekends to look after the gardens."

"Who looked after Toby?"

BODY PARTS

"My neighbour."

"How long did you work for Lord and Lady Hasford?"

"Until Lord Hasford died."

"So why did you leave?"

"Well to be open an honest, me and Lady Hasford didn't get on. She always wanted rid of me and she was looking for an excuse to sack me. So I left, I wasn't giving her the pleasure."

"Could I ask you how old you are?"

"I'm fifty three."

"What jobs have you had?"

"I was an engineer in the army. Then when I came out I worked on the oil rigs in Scotland. When Andrea died in childbirth I came back to the Peak District. I have worked for many years as a Park Ranger for the Peak Park."

"So, I will ask you again, did you know the first victim Alan Hewitt?"

"No, I didn't."

"What about the second victim, Larry Bailey?"

"Yes, my half-brother."

"The third victim, DCI Dirk?"

"No comment."

"By that I assume you didn't know him."

Again Glew said no comment.

"Ok, victim number four, Raitus Esmar, did you know this man?"

"No."

"Ok, just a few more questions. Have you any experience working with knives?"

"I was a chef in the army."

"Ok, I think we have enough to be getting on with Mr Glew, we may need to speak again."

BODY PARTS

At this point Broome stood up looking all aggressive.

"Should you wish to speak with my client again, a formal complaint will be sent from my office, DCI Gammon."

Gammon indicated to Milton to cut the tape.

"Let me assure you Mr Broome, I have four dead bodies and a police officer missing. If you for one minute think threatening me with a formal complaint will stop me executing my duties you are very mistaken. Good day," and Gammon left the room with Broome looking aghast at the other officers.

Gammon was fuming and went straight to his office. With the cameras up at his house he trawled the images to see if he could see anybody, but there was nothing. Gammon decided to go and see Lady

Hasford at Parwich Hall to chat to her about John Glew. He wanted her version of events.

John arrived at Pritwich. He parked his car on the side of the road and walked up the steps, which were well worn, the building had been in place since 1673 with bits added to it. The Hasford crest was above the arched gate way. John could see little Rosie playing on a swing at the far end. He was hoping she wouldn't see him in case she asked about her mum. John just didn't know what to say. Lady Hasford's maid came to the door.

"DCI Gammon, is Lady Hasford available?"

"Just a minute Mr Gammon, I will let her know you are here."

"John, do come in."

BODY PARTS

Lady Hasford was quite a striking lady. John could see where Sandra got her looks and decorum from.

"Have you any news?"

"No, I am afraid not, but you could help me with a few questions."

"Yes, anything John."

Lady Hasford asked the maid to make a pot of tea, and as she put it some fancies. John took that to mean cake.

"Follow me into the drawing room."

The oak panelled drawing room had oil painting of Sandra's ancestors neatly displayed on the panelling with a small picture light over each one.

They sat down and Gammon began with his questions.

"I have interviewed a man who is of concern to us today, and I wondered if you could help me."

"But of course."

"The man's name is John Glew. Does that mean anything to you?"

"Yes, I'm afraid it does. Lord Hasford acquired him to do gardening chores when he was alive. I believe I am a good judge of character and I really didn't trust him."

"In what way?"

"Every way, John. A few years ago we had been on a cruise and our maid at the time said she would sleep in the big house while we were away. She was pretty thing; her name was Alice Roberts. We had been to Egypt for three weeks, you know cruising the Nile, like so many people do these days. When we got back Mr Glew met us and carried our cases into the hallway. I shouted for Alice but that's when Glew said she had left. Alice had worked for me for almost thirty years and the most compassionate and trustworthy person I have ever met."

"This concerned me, and I asked Mr Glew why she had left. His revelation shocked me. He said he had caught her taking jewellery from my bedroom."

"Did he have proof of that, Lady Hasford?"

"No, he did not, but he said that Alice had said if he told my husband and I, she would say he had tried to rape her. Then he said two days later she told him she was leaving."

"She had come from Scotland and had worked in London before coming to me with excellent references. She never spoke about any family, she was a very private person. I'm afraid I never saw her again."

"Did you report it to the police?"

"No I didn't, because Lord Hasford said it would all be investigated and would bring shame on our good name. He would never allow that."

"Many years later when Sandra came back to live in Pritwich she asked about Alice, just in general conversation. She said she remembered Alice as a lovely person. So, you see Mr Gammon, myself and my daughter can't be wrong."

The maid arrived with a china tea pot and cups and some small salmon and cucumber sandwiches with the crusts cut off. Also ham and beef with horseradish sandwiches presented the same. There was also a beautiful china cake stand with fairy buns, small Victoria sandwich cakes, walnut and date slices and strawberry meringues.

BODY PARTS

"Wow, this is very good of you Lady Hasford."

"It's nice to have some company, it takes my mind off the situation."

"How is Rosie coping?"

"I have told her Sandra is away on Police business, but will be back soon. I could hardly tell her the truth, could I?"

"No, very difficult, Lady Hasford."

John polished of a good third of the sandwiches and cake and thanked Lady Hasford for the information and hospitality. He turned to her as he left.

"I will find who has got Sandra, Lady Hasford."

The poor woman just looked at John with hope in her steely blue eyes.

John walked down the path and Rosie spotted him. She waved furiously and shouted, "Hello John."

This made it worse. John's mind was racing, what if this nutter had dismembered Sandra?

He needed a drink and headed for the Spinning Jenny and Kev. It was 6.10pm and the place was packed but no sign of Kev. Tracey Rodgers was behind the bar with Carol Lestar.

"Be with you in a minute, John," Carol hollered down the bar like only Carol could do.

Eventually with the traffic at bar decreased and Carol came to serve him.

"Pedigree, John?"

"Yes please, Carol. What's all this about?"

"Dilley Dale end of season boules party."

"Funny night for that, Carol. Where's Kev?"

BODY PARTS

"They have gone to look at a house in Puddle Dale. I think they forgot about all this or they wouldn't have left us. I suppose their minds are on retirement."

"Not sure, Doreen will ever properly retire, she is always on the go. Now Kev on the other hand, he has got his retirement worked out with holidays and the races, he can't wait. Just excuse me, best get some more served. Oh, by the way, Mum is so much better John. You must pop and see her. I will always be grateful."

"Not a problem as long as she is on the mend."

John stood at the corner of the bar watching the boules lot having a good time, when there was a tap on his shoulder. It was a small man in a three-piece suit and tie and small John Lennon type glasses. To be fair John hadn't got a clue who he was.

"Hey, John Gammon, lovely to see you. I heard you had moved up to Derbyshire, didn't we, Mary?" the man said to a small lady in her late sixties.

"Yes, our boy lives in Cramford."

"Oh really, well small world eh."

John still had no idea who he was talking to. The man asked John if he could remember Arthur Sykes.

"Nasty do that was, John."

It suddenly hit John like a sledge hammer. The man he was talking to was Pedantic Pete Club. He was DI Club when he served in London with him.

"Bloody hell Peter, how you doing?"

"I thought you were struggling to recognise me. I've put a bit of weight on since I retired three years back and I heard you were still up here."

BODY PARTS

"No, sorry mate, got so much on my plate at the minute."

"So what dizzy heights have you achieved up here mate?"

"I'm DCI at Bixton."

"Well done lad, you always were destined for the top."

"Give over you old bugger, excuse my French, Mrs Club."

"Heard worse, John," and she laughed. John got Peter a double whisky and Mrs Club a large white wine.

They stood together reminiscing for almost three hours before John said he best make a move.

"Lovely to see you lad, and pleased you are doing well, you were always destined for the top."

Peter shook John's hand and wished him all the best.

John arrived home and poured himself a big glass of Jameson's before opening his lap top to quickly look at the camera recordings To John's amazement there was nothing but a black screen. He wasn't sure if it was his computer, the camera or his screen. John grabbed his torch to check the camera, and to his surprise the lens had been painted black. It was still a bit tacky, so it hadn't been done that long. This person or persons are playing with me he thought.

Another week passed with no word on Sandra Scooper or from the person or persons that may have abducted her.

Gammon arrived at the station to be greeted by the new DI Katy Bass. Katy had been fast tracked with her university degrees. She was clearly bright and well thought of so Gammon was pleased with his choice.

"Come up to my office Katy, and we can have a coffee, and I can fill you in your new position as a DS at Bixton."

"Thank you, Sir," Katy replied.

Gammon got two coffees and explained what was expected from Katy in her new position as Detective Sergeant.

"We are a solid team here in Bixton."

"I have heard a lot about you, Sir."

"I hope all good, Katy," and Gammon laughed.

"Now I have filled you in on the cases we are working on I will take you round to introduce you to the team."

Katy was a bit nervous but was confident her abilities would get her through.

Series Three
Book Three
in the John Gammon Detective Series

Gammon took DS Bass into see Milton, Smarty and Lee. Milton's eye lit up when he saw Katy.

"This our new DS Katy Bass, gentlemen. She has joined us from Cambridge, but she is a local girl so that knowledge should help in the cases we tackle."

Gammon then he introduced her to PC Magic. He knew it may be awkward as basically Kate had taken what was his position. Gammon was pleased with Magic's professionalism. He wished her all the best.

Gammon took Kate down to meet John Walvin's crew.

"Ok Kate, I'll take you back up and IT should have you sorted in the office with Lee, Smarty and DI Milton. These are all good officers and you will learn a lot from them."

BODY PARTS

Kate smiled, she had already spotted DI Milton looking at her longingly. She wasn't sure how that might play out in the coming months. With the team introduced Gammon took Kate for a coffee in Bixton to give her a feel for the place.

"So, Kate do you have family in the area still?"

"Oh yes, that was one of the reasons I decided to come back. My Aunty Sheba lives locally, so I am stopping with her until I get sorted."

"Never, Sheba Filey?"

"Yes, do you know her?"

"Yes, I do actually and her boyfriend Phil Sterndale."

"Oh, I haven't met Phil yet, but I know she seems really happy with him."

"Yes, they appear to make a good couple."

"So, how well do you know Aunty Sheba, Sir?"

"Oh, quite well. Her parents were farmers and mine were, but really got to know her through Jack and Shelley Etchings."

"Jack and Shelley, aren't they lovely and their family?"

"Yes, nice people, Kate."

"So, what's the position with our missing colleague, Sir?"

"DI Scooper. Sandra is a real valued member of the team, and she was abducted at Alford in the Water. It appeared she got out of her car to help somebody. It was a ghastly night, and she hasn't been seen since. The person or persons doing the killings that we are investigating, I believe has her."

"That's terrible, Sir."

BODY PARTS

"Yes, not good Kate."

"Well I am pleased you have somewhere to stay. B and B's can be soulless places if you stay too long."

"I can imagine, Sir. Can I ask you a question, Sir?"

"Yes, anything Kate, fire away."

"I know this will sound silly, but how do you cope with the pressure your name carries?"

"Not sure I know what you mean."

"Well everybody I spoke to has said there isn't a better copper in the force, and you always get your man. I know the people of the Peak District are in debt to you for the arrests you have made."

"It's all part of the job I love Kate, so I don't stand much stall to it I guess."

Gammon's phone rang. It was Steve.

Series Three
Book Three
in the John Gammon Detective Series

"Hey mate, wondered if you fancied coming down to the Star tonight? Not seen you for a bit."

"Yes, can do mate, what time?"

"Well Imogen is open all day. She is really making a go of it, so when you finish work if you want?"

"Sounds good to me mate, will see you about 5.30pm."

"Look forward to it, John," and Steve hung up.

"Ok Kate, we best get back."

Gammon took Kate back and Milton was fussing round her which made Gammon smile.

Gammon left spot on 5.00pm to go and see Steve at The Star in Puddle Dale. Puddle Dale was absolutely fabulous at this time of year. It was a particularly large village, but very old and quaint. John parked his car and went inside. Steve was sitting at the bar talking to Imogen. There were three walkers sitting in the corner with what looked like cheese and onion cobs and three pints half drank.

"Hey mate, how are you?"

"I'm good Steve, how are you?"

"Very good mate. Me and Imogen wanted you to be the first to know."

"Oh yeah, know what mate?"

"We are getting engaged."

Although John was shocked, he wasn't surprised. Steve had always been impulsive, right since early school days.

"Oh, if that's what you want, I am pleased for you."

"I know it might seem early mate, but Jo would have wanted me to be happy."

Imogen just stood smiling like she had won the lottery.

"So, what about the house and land mate, are you still going to build it back to its former glory?"

"No, we are going to buy this place. I know it's early days, but I can't drag that behind me for the rest of my life. Jo would have wanted me to move on."

Any wonder Imogen was looking pleased John thought.

"Come on mate, what are you having?"

"You should try this, it's called Puddle Dale Surprise. It flippin' surprised me last night. I had all on getting to bed, didn't I Imogen?"

"You always were a lightweight, Lineman," and John laughed.

BODY PARTS

He was pleased his mate was on the road back. He just hoped he wasn't rushing things with Imogen

The Star pub was quite busy and a credit to Imogen the food looked excellent. She was a smart girl with big plans for the business.

John just ordered another drink when his mobile rang. It was Di Trimble.

"Sir, sorry to bother you, but we have just had a letter delivered for your attention. It looks very much like the previous ones that were left at your house."

"Ok Di, I'll pop back."

"Steve, sorry mate, duty calls. Tell Imogen thanks for asking me over and I will give you a call."

"Ok John, see you soon."

Gammon left and headed straight back to Bixton.

Series Three
Book Three
in the John Gammon Detective Series

Di Trimble had been on the desk on night shift for many years and she was a good copper in Gammon's eyes. He knew if she called him it was most probably very important.

"Evening Di."

"Congratulations on your promotion Sir, should have happened ages ago."

"Thanks Di, appreciate your support. So, what have we got Di and how was it delivered?"

"That's just it, Sir. It was left there on the small desk where you come in. I didn't see anybody arrive with it."

"Ok Di, well let me have a read and then I can take a look at the CCTV tape."

Trimble handed DCI Gammon the envelope addressed to him. Gammon carefully opened the envelope.

BODY PARTS

'Good evening John

Sorry if my little note ruined your evening but I know you like to keep things in an orderly manner.

You will find the body of Helen Spirios wife of Dimitri Spirios who owns the fish and chip shop in Rowksly.

Dear Dimitri, he is a nice man, but his wife could be a little on the arrogant side shall we say so I don't think Rowksly will miss her. I chopped her up very neatly and kept the parts I wanted. You will find her in a bin liner in the Junior School Playground at Monkdale. I was going to leave it until morning but felt it wasn't right with little children playing there in the morning.

Anyway, best crack on I have a lot to do until we meet my friend.

Frank Stein.'

"Di, get Wally and his team over to Monkdale Junior school. There is a body in a bin liner and I don't want anybody else finding it. Phone Margaret Bradbury. I would like to meet her here also. Send DI Smarty, DI Lee and DS Bass to the scene. I want them questioning anybody that may have seen somebody dumping a bin liner in the school playground."

"I'm on it now, Sir."

Gammon went off to look at the tape to see if anybody showed placing the letter at the front table.

He sat for almost two hours when a scruffy looking man in tracksuit bottoms and a long straggly beard appeared on the tape. He came into the station entrance and was looking around before he placed the letter on the table turned and left. The outside cameras appeared to show him on foot.

Gammon printed off two pictures; one showing the size of the man and the other a close up of his face which actually was quite good. Gammon then set about trawling the Police Database for matches. By now Margaret Bradbury had arrived and John showed her the pictures.

"Well it appears he is working alone, John. But something isn't right. Look at his shoes, sorry trainers, they look quite new, but he looks dishevelled."

"Good spot, Margaret," Gammon said peering over the computer.

"Are you having any luck on the database?"

"Nothing yet, Margaret."

Almost four hours passed when DS Bass, DI Lee and DI Smarty got back.

Series Three
Book Three
in the John Gammon Detective Series

"Have you got anything?"

"Not sure, DS Bass spotted a guy hanging around. She questioned him, and he said he saw somebody with a bag."

"Did he see their face?"

"No, he said they had a motorbike helmet on. But he did say it was a Black AGV."

Bass looked at her notes.

"Sorry Sir, an AGV helmet Black K3-SV. He said he knew it was because he used to have one when he had his motorbike."

"Good work, DS Bass."

"Ok everybody, thanks for coming in. Let's call it a night and reconvene in the incident room at 9.00am."

They all left, and Gammon walked out with Margaret Bradbury.

BODY PARTS

"This could be the killer's first mistake, John."

"I certainly hope so, Margaret."

"Is everything still good at Jim and Lisa's place."

"Oh, yes John, I love it. Lisa is so good, nothing is too much trouble for her, really makes me feel welcome."

"Good, ok goodnight Margaret. See you in the morning."

Gammon drove back to his cottage thinking it had been a strange evening. His best mate had got engaged and then the letter and the body were found.

John poured a large Jameson's and headed for his bed, mindful that this could well mean they had a lead at last.

John slept well, and his alarm woke him up which was unusual. He showered and shaved and headed down to the kitchen for a coffee. John almost dropped his coffee in shock. On the table was a 6" x 9" picture of Sandra in a white plastic frame on his table. This meant somebody had broken in during the night while he was asleep upstairs. On the back of the photograph was a typed note which simply said, *'Until we meet again John'*

John drove to work and on the way he was thinking that never in all the years he had been in the police had anybody been so blatantly playing games with him. It was like he wanted to be caught.

John arrived just before 9.00am and the whole team were already and waiting.

"Ok thanks for last night, those of you who were called out. Before we go much further, we have good pictures from the CCTV tape that shows this bearded man dropping off the letter. We have a witness who states he saw a man in a bike helmet drop something in the school playground. So, first thing after this meeting, all take a real good look at the man in question."

"DS Bass, you check if any of the suspects that we have questioned own or have ever owned a motorbike."

"DI Milton you help Kate with this please."

"Ok, Margaret, have you anything to add?"

"Personally, I think the guy dropping the letter is a red herring, but the motorbike guy could be our man."

"Wally, what have you for us on the body?"

"Well, we had little to look at; no arms or legs, just a torso and a head, but the head had been separated from the torso. It appears that the head was severed, and for some reason whoever is doing this changed their mind, and left it with the torso. But we have had one stroke of luck. We found some blood on the torso which isn't that of the victim, but most probably that of the assailant."

"Have you checked the database, Wally?"

"No, one of the girls in the lab is on that now."

"Whatever the result, good or bad, I need to know immediately."

"With regard to any connections to motorbikes and our suspects I want to know about that immediately. Finally, I was broken into again last night and left this present."

He showed the team the picture and the words on the back.

BODY PARTS

"Sir, that picture was taken at the Spinning Jenny by the Micklock Mercury when we arrested the Alison boy, remember?"

"How can I forget? That was one we made a total bollocks of by charging him. Perhaps this is something else this nut case is trying to say?"

"Ok, DI Lee call at the Micklock Mercury office and see what pictures have been ordered from the last two months, but please be discreet. Last thing I need is the press boys crawling all over us, Peter."

"Ok, Sir."

Wally confirmed the deceased lady was indeed Helen Spirios from Rowksly chip shop. Gammon decided to drive out and see Mr Spirios with the bad news.

Series Three
Book Three
in the John Gammon Detective Series

Rowksly was a pretty village and the
Spirios family had come over from Cyprus
some twenty years before to settle in
Rowksly. They had bought the fish and
chip shop from Annie Blackham, a village
character who had ran it for almost fifty
years. In those days all Annie sold was fish
and chips with mushy peas or gravy,
nothing else. John remembered cycling on
a Saturday night with his brother Adam for
Annie's fish and chips. They would be
queuing from 5.30pm until she shut at
9.30pm, and people came from far and
wide. Spirios changed things a bit bringing
in Kebabs and things, but times move on
John thought.

Spirios wasn't open when he arrived, so
Gammon went around to the side and
followed the path to the rear door. Dimitri

was sitting with a coffee stroking his springer spaniel whilst enjoying the view.

"Mr Spirios."

"Oh hello, Mr Gammon, we are not open yet," he said in broken English.

"Could I have a word, Mr Spirios?"

"What have I done? Is it about the liquor licence?"

"No, Mr Spirios. I am afraid I have some bad news for you."

"Bad news, Mr Gammon?"

"I'm afraid your wife has been found murdered at Monkdale late last night."

Dimitri looked shocked.

"How you mean murdered?"

"I am afraid she was dismembered and left in a black bin liner in Monkdale Primary school yard."

"Who would do this?"

Dimitri looked shocked at John's revelation.

"Why my wife, Mr Gammon?"

"I wish I had the answers, Mr Spirios. Do you have family I can contact?"

"Only my brother in Cyprus."

"What about children?"

"We no have children."

"Does Mrs Spirios have family?"

"No, all gone now."

"Look Mr Spirios, I can arrange for somebody to come over for you at this delicate stage."

"No, I am fine, Mr Gammon. I have business to run."

Gammon had to admire the strength of the man.

"Could I ask you to identify your wife's body tomorrow?"

"Yes, I come and see, Mr Gammon."

BODY PARTS

"Here is my card, I may want to speak with you at some point Dimitri."

"This is ok, Mr Gammon."

Gammon could see Dimitri wanted to open the fish and chip shop to take his mind off things.

"If you are sure you are ok, Mr Spirios?"

Dimitri nodded and went through the back and into the shop. Gammon walked back round to his car thinking what a proud man Dimitri Spirios was holding his emotions in like that.

Gammon headed back to the station and his pile of paperwork which had now grown unbelievably in his new position as DCI.

Gammon grabbed a coffee and stood for five minutes looking to Losehill. It always seemed to help his thinking, and his thoughts were on Sandra. Whoever was doing these killings had Sandra for a reason. She wasn't just a random snatch, he didn't think.

Gammon slowly started working down his mail when the phone rang.

"I have Sir Gavin Boomer from the Home Office on the line."

"Ok Magic, thanks."

"DCI Gammon, how can I help?"

"Gavin Boomer," said the voice on the other end of the line.

"We need results, Gammon, performance at Bixton is abysmal. How many murders is it now currently unsolved? And we also have Detective Inspector apparently being held. I have arranged for a news conference up here in London tomorrow, and you must attend. It will be in the Kilburn House Hotel in Pall Mall. The news boys said it will be live at

BODY PARTS

11.00 am, so you must be here by 9.30am to meet me and Chief Constable Andrew Sim from Derbyshire Police. This isn't a request DCI Gammon, this is an order. Good day," and Boomer slammed down the phone.

Gammon was fuming, this pompous idiot can have my job he thought. How dare he tell me that my station is not performing. Just then Margaret Bradbury appeared at Gammon's door.

"Looking a bit annoyed, Mr Gammon?"

"Oh, I have been summoned to London by some pompous idiot, Sir Gavin Boomer."

"Know him well. He has turned brown-nosing into an art form, John. Watch yourself with him. If he is involved I am guessing the press boys are as well, because he likes the sound of his own voice."

"Great Margaret, that's all I need."

Gammon's door opened again.

"Sorry to interrupt Sir, but think we have found the guy who delivered the letter. His name is Harold Mackay. Magic remembered seeing him. He sits begging outside Boots in Bixton. DI Milton has gone to bring him in."

"Brilliant. DI Smarty, put him in interview room one and get him a solicitor. When it's organised come and get me."

"Will do, Sir."

Gammon was now feeling the pressure. He needed this guy to be part of the jigsaw. Two hours passed before Milton arrived with the guy. Gammon went down to the interview room. Inside were DI Milton, duty solicitor, Tony Rara, and the suspect.

BODY PARTS

Gammon got a distinct whiff of alcohol. Milton introduced everyone to the tape and Gammon sat opposite the man. He thought he must have been about thirty eight, but because he slept rough and didn't look after himself he looked nearer seventy. Gammon wasn't sure about what use he would be.

"Could I have your name please?"

"They call me Hogbreath."

"Really?"

Gammon couldn't help himself.

"Good name, ain't it?"

"But what is your correct name?"

"Harold Mackay," and he laughed showing his rotten teeth, well what was left of them.

"Ok, so where do you live?"

"Boots on the High Street in Bixton."

"So, you sleep rough, correct?"

Series Three
Book Three
in the John Gammon Detective Series

"Yeah, whatever you want to call it is fine by me."

"Mr Mackay, we have footage of you placing a letter on a table in the entrance to Bixton Police Station. Did you write that letter?"

"No, I didn't. A man offered me two hundred pounds to deliver it to the Police Station, which I did."

"Mr Mackay, what did the man look like?"

"I couldn't tell, he was wearing a crash helmet."

"Do you know the seriousness of your actions?"

"Look, let me explain something to you. I'm not a half-wit. I may smell because I can't bath or shower. I have a degree in law, so I am well versed in what my actions could lead to. But when you are hungry and cold, then what is the worst you can do to me? Lock me up in a warm cell, give me three meals a day and let me shower. It sounds like a fair swap to me."

Gammon understood what he was saying but he wanted to dig a bit deeper.

"So, the guy who gave you the letter, was there anything unusual about him? Was he tall, small, fat, thin? Did he have a limp or anything distinguishing, maybe a tattoo?"

"My hearing isn't great, and he did mumble. I think he may have been foreign, but I'm not sure. He was about my height."

"Which is what? Stand up Mr Mackay. For the tape I would suggest around five feet nine."

"He also carried some weight."

"Anything else?"

"No, that's all I know."

Series Three
Book Three
in the John Gammon Detective Series

"Do you have any of the two hundred pounds left that we could look at?"

Gammon was thinking there maybe DNA, or they could trace it through the actual bank note number. Mackay fiddled about in his pocket and pulled out sixty pounds and placed it on the table.

"Right, we will look at this, and the front desk will give you a receipt for it."

"And pray, what do you suggest I buy food with tonight?"

Gammon opened his wallet and gave him sixty pounds.

"I will now sign for the money, Mr Mackay."

"I don't have any further questioning at this time, but I suggest you don't move on, as there may be further questions at some point."

BODY PARTS

"You will always find me at Boots. Good day to you," he said, and he left.

Gammon turned to DI Milton.

"Guess we at least have some kind of lead. Get everyone together in the incident room Carl, and let's see what we have. I am in London tomorrow at a press conference, so would like to take some information with me."

With everyone assembled Gammon informed everyone what Harold Mackay had said.

"Look, I'm not sure how reliable this guy is. He was clearly an intelligent man that lost his way, but he did smell of booze so he could be just saying anything."

"Mackay said the man that paid him two hundred pounds to deliver the letter was stout, about five feet nine in height and the interesting thing he said he thought he may have been foreign."

Just then Magic came in.

"Sir, Harold Mackay has just come back and said the man's crash helmet was black, but he noticed the word 'IRON' transferred on the back."

"Ok thanks, Magic."

"Well, maybe this guy is credible. Ok DS Bass what have you managed to find out?"

"Well, all three suspects have owned motorbikes would you believe? John Glew still owns one. Peter Scarthin still owns one and Toby Glew is no longer the registered keeper. He apparently sold his two days ago to Pedro Kuna who he works with him at the Meat Warehouse."

"Great, well done Kate. You and DI Smarty go round and see these guys, also the foreign guy who Toby Glew sold the bike to and check their helmets."

"Sir."

"Yes, DI Lee."

"None of the suspects you would say are overweight."

"Doesn't mean anything, Peter. It was probably done as some kind of disguise, as was possibly the foreign brogue that Mackay thought the man spoke."

"Right everyone I have a news conference in London to attend tomorrow, so I am going to set off now and stay down there."

CAPTER SIX

Gammon left for London. He had managed to get a room for the night at the Kilburn House Hotel. John took the train arriving at 8.00pm. He knew London well from his time down there. He thought about calling Andrew Sim to see if he wanted to meet up, but then thought he wouldn't want to spend any more time than needed with Gavin Boomer. John quickly showered and decided to try a pub he frequented when he was a young rookie cop. The pub called Losers Hand was quite some place, and he wondered how much it had changed. He got the taxi to drop him off. From the outside it hadn't changed much, but inside it was packed with waiters bringing food out. Most of the pub was taken up with dining. So much different from the old stale cobs in a glass case on the bar and now with no smoking that thick haze had gone, it was a totally different place. John decided on a meal which he could see from the food coming out of the kitchen was really good.

Once the meal was eaten he called for a taxi and headed back to the hotel. He was just about to go to his room when he noticed DI Smarty sat in the Foyer.

"Dave, what are you doing here?" Gammon noticed Dave Smarty had two large glasses of brandy on the table.

"Are you on a bender lad," he said laughing.

"Sit down John, this is serious."

"What's serious?"

"I wanted to tell you personally."

"Tell me what, Dave?"

"It's Sandra Scooper, John. She has been murdered and her head was found on the bonnet of your car as I was leaving work."

Smarty could not control his emotion any longer and tears flooded down his cheeks like a storm gate had been opened.

"I am so sorry mate, she was a lovely girl."

John immediately drank the double brandy and with his voice quivering he said.

"Where is the rest of her body?"

"It was found propped against your front door."

"Why didn't anybody call me?"

"I told them not to. I knew how close you both were, so I wanted to tell you myself," Smarty said crying into his handkerchief.

"Dave, what the hell is this all about?"

BODY PARTS

"I don't know John, but this is one sick guy."

"What about poor Rosie?"

"Look, do you want me to do the conference tomorrow?"

"No Dave, I will have to do it. You go back."

Smarty made sure John was ok and left him. John wanted to get drunk, but he knew he had to hold it together for the press conference the following day. John made himself a strong coffee and lay on the king size bed. He didn't want to be in London, not now, he wanted to get home.

John stared at the ceiling tears rolling down his face thinking about the good times him and Sandra had over the years. They would laugh, and she was always there for him. They kept things professional at work, but out of work he knew she loved him. But he could never commit, and he knew she found it really hard at times. He also knew that she supported him with Saron, and was the first one there when he was very ill and Annie Tanney saved his life. All these things were swirling round John's head.

Chief Constable Andrew Sim was waiting in reception.

"Are you ok John? You don't look well. Are you coming down with something?"

"It's DI Scooper Sir. She has been murdered and the sick monster chopped her head off and delivered it to Bixton Police Station on my car bonnet. Her body was found propped at my cottage door. He is sending signals, Sir."

BODY PARTS

"Oh dear John, I am very sorry. I know DI Scooper was a trusted member of your team, that is dreadful."

Gavin Bloomer arrived.

"Sorry about the delay, just had the PM on. He is wanting me to pop round to number ten once these boys have been pacified, which I hope Gammon will address seeing that it's on his patch."

Gammon looked at Sim. He really wanted to punch bloody Gavin Boomer.

"Right, let's get in there. I have golf at lunchtime with the Defence Secretary."

The more Gammon listened to this prick the more he despised him.

All the press were there and Sky News, ITV news and BBC World News. Flashbulbs started firing off as they walked up to the table set on a makeshift stage. Sir Gavin Bloomer introduced himself, Chief

Series Three
Book Three
in the John Gammon Detective Series

Constable Sim and then turned to Gammon and said this is DCI John Gammon from Bixton Police Station he will take your questions. Talk about throw the underling under the bus.

The questions started.

"Mike Dixon, Sky News. DCI Gammon, how do you go about settling the concerns of the people in the Peak District with the current amount of five butchered victims, and one serving police officer? You are no further forward catching this maniac." Gammon felt a lump in his throat. He didn't want to tell the media Sandra was dead. He was hoping to tell Sandra's mother himself, but now he had no choice.

"First of all," Gammon said clearing his throat. "We at Bixton have great sadness in our hearts today. I was given the news last night that DI Sandra Scooper had also been murdered by, as you term it, this maniac."

There was silence in the room. Gavin Bloomer was shocked.

"Harry Lyme, Micklock Mercury. DCI Gammon, how was DI Scooper murdered? How have you linked that to the other five victims?"

"I'm afraid I can't divulge that at this time, not until I have looked at it myself."

John didn't want to go into the gruesome details of Sandra's death to the media pack.

"Bill Wickman, BBC World Service. So, you now have six victims, have you any suspects."

"We are questioning several people who we suspect could have knowledge of the crimes."

"Who are they DI Gammon? Are they local men?"

Series Three
Book Three
in the John Gammon Detective Series

"Again, I can't comment on this with it being an ongoing case. What I will tell you is we do have an eye witness which hopefully will lead to something concrete."

The questions became more personal and Gammon was feeling more aggravated every time poor Sandra's name was mentioned. It had now been almost an hour and Sir Gavin Bloomer was looking at his watch, so Chief Constable Andrew Sim intervened.

"Ok gents, that's as much as we are prepared to talk on these cases. I trust you will respect that DCI Gammon wishes to get back to Bixton after the loss of a close colleague."

Gammon, Sim and Boomer stood up with a barrage of flashlight firing off simultaneously in their direction.

BODY PARTS

They left through a back-door. Andrew Sim took Gammon back to the train station. Gavin Boomer never asked after Sandra, he was more concerned with his golf game.

"If you need anything John, as I am guessing losing Sandra, you will need another officer."

"Thank you, Sir."

"Listen, I have other business in London so will be here all week, but you have my number."

"Thank you, Sir."

"Please give my condolences to Sandra's family and her colleagues at Bixton Station."

"I will Sir, and thank you."

John caught his train. He sat opposite a woman with a young child no more than a year old. His mind wandered to his little girl Anka Emily. How was he going to play this? He knew if Saron ever found out, any chance of them being a couple would be scuppered. He didn't want to chance that, but he would love to be a part of Anka's life in the future.

The train pulled into Bixton station and John had rang DI Smarty to pick him up.

"Afternoon John, how are you?"

"Feeling beat up."

"Well I hope you don't mind, but I went and told DI Scoopers mother of her tragic loss."

"I was pushed in a corner mate. I didn't want to announce Sandra's death on live TV, but I had no choice."

"Well you are ok, her mum hadn't heard the news."

"How was she, Dave?"

BODY PARTS

"In bits mate, but that was to be expected. She now has to bring up young Rosie on her own, which will be hard at her age."

"Thanks for that mate."

"No bother, John."

Dave dropped John at the station to get his car.

"Do you want a quick beer, Dave?"

"No, I best get back mate, wife goes to a craft class tonight."

"Sounds like fun, mate."

"Yeah, we will have to try it sometime. See you in the morning John."

"Goodnight Dave."

John headed to the Spinning Jenny he needed a drink. The bar was quite full including Bob, Cheryl and her partner Jackie, Phil Sterndale and Sheba, Jimmy

Lowcee was talking to Carol Lestar. They went quiet when John walked in. Sheba came straight over and hugged John.

"So sorry about Sandra, John."

"Thanks, Sheba."

By the time he got to order a drink all the girls had hugged him telling him how sorry they were.

John ordered everybody a drink. Then stood talking to Carol and Jimmy.

"So, are the rumours true?"

"What's that then, John?"

"That you are buying the Spinning Jenny?"

"Don't know yet. I think there are three couples in for it since we said we were interested."

"Oh wow, it's a popular pub though and the food is excellent."

BODY PARTS

"Yeah, if we get it we are going to put theme nights on, aren't we Jimmy?"

"That's what you tell me," Jimmy said wiping the top of his bottle with so much vivacity that John thought he was polishing it.

"Do you know John, I have lived here all my life, and for the first time I am worried about walking my little dog at night. What a terrible year we have had first Jo and the baby die in that fire now Sandra Scooper has been murdered, it's dreadful."

John really couldn't talk about Sandra, so he made his excuses and wandered over to Jack and Shelly.

"How are you lad?"

"Oh, I'm ok Jack, bit shook up about Sandra, but I guess we all are."

"Yes, she was a nice lass. Just hope you get the idiot that is doing this John."

Series Three
Book Three
in the John Gammon Detective Series

"I promise you I will Jack, Sandra meant a lot to me."

By 9.30pm John had enough so he left quietly and returned to his cottage, He showered and got in bed with his book. That was some day he thought.

The following day John spoke with Chief Constable Andrew Sim about Sandra's funeral, and if she was to have a full police funeral. Sim said she was, and that he would also like to attend. Andrew Sim asked John if he knew her well enough to do a eulogy.

"Of course Sir, it would be an honour."

Gammon sat in his office doodling on his writing pad when Wally knocked on his door.

"Hi Wally."

BODY PARTS

"I have found something on Sandra's body, John."

"You have what?"

"There is a distinct smell of fish. She had been somewhere where there was fish."

"Right thanks, Wally."

Gammon picked up the phone and called Smarty and Milton.

"Take DI Lee and DS Bass and search every warehouse or building that may stock fish," and he explained what Wally had told him.

"I would like a full report and a meeting in the incident room by 9.00am. Also tell DS Bass I want the information on the Biker helmets for the morning."

"Oh, and Dave, has DS Winnipeg come back to work yet?"

"Think he is due back in a couple of days."

"Bloody hell, we haven't seen him yet, have we?"

"No, he came off his motorbike the day before his start, so not been introduced or anything."

"Ok, remind me when he does come to work Dave, so that I can go round and formally introduce him."

"Will do, John."

It was 11.00 am when John finally plucked up the courage to go and see Sandra's mother about the funeral arrangements. This was something he really wasn't looking forward to as he walked up to knock on the front door of the hall.

John was shown into the study where Lady Hasford was sitting.

"Oh, good morning, John."

"Good morning, Lady Hasford."

BODY PARTS

She immediately stood up and hugged John which quite took John by surprise.

"I am at a loss of what to do, John. At my age I have to bring little Rosie up, and to be honest, I had looked for some time about going to live in the Scilly Isles. This place is too big for me and I only have Rosie left to leave everything too now So before she goes to upper school the time is right to move on."

"Are you sure Lady Hasford? These are big decisions to make, and maybe while you are grieving this isn't a good time."

"No John, I have made my mind up. I have an estate agent coming this afternoon. The funeral director is coming tonight to see me, so I will call you with the arrangements for Sandra's funeral."

"How was Rosie?"

Series Three
Book Three
in the John Gammon Detective Series

"She seems ok, but who knows what is going through her little mind, John?"

"How are you, John?"

"Yes, I'm ok."

"Sandra didn't tell me an awful lot. We never really had that kind of relationship, but I do know she thought an awful lot of you."

"The feeling was mutual Lady Hasford. One of the reasons I am here is my Chief Constable Andrew Sim wishes to give Sandra a full police funeral, if you are ok with that?"

"Yes, she loved her job, John."

"Well she certainly deserves this from the Police and her colleagues. Ok Lady Hasford, give me a call when you know the dates and I will speak with Andrew Sim about the police involvement."

BODY PARTS

With that John left Lady Hasford thumbing through Country Life estates.

On the way back John's phone rang, it was Saron.

"Hi John, I have just heard about Sandra. We weren't the best of mates for obvious reasons, but I did like her and her poor little girl. How is she?"

"I have just left Lady Hasford. She is moving to the Scilly Isles. I told her it's a bit early to make such a life changing decision, but she is adamant."

"It's probably shock John, must be terrible for her. Can you imagine if you had a daughter, how you would feel never seeing her again?"

John hated lying but he just went along with Saron's sentiments. He already knew what it was like not to see his daughter.

Back at the station PC Magic asked if he could have a word. Gammon told him to ask another PC to watch the front desk and told him to come to his office.

"Now then Magic, what's the problem?"

"Well I have two problems, Sir. I'm not sure I can handle this desk job. I like to be involved, and it pretty much looks like I have cooked my goose in the Police Force."

Gammon didn't comment.

"So what's your second point?"

"Well, I have a friend from way back that lives in Rowksly. You know the lady that was murdered by this maniac we are hunting, Mrs Spirios. My friend tells me she is a bit of a lass, or should I say was a bit of a lass."

"Explain yourself, Magic."

BODY PARTS

"Helen Spirios was a stunning Greek woman, cracking figure, long dark hair, she looked like Sophie Loren. My friend said when they first moved in the village all the locals were sniffing round her. He said Spirios had a temper. One day my friend was stood waiting for his fish to cook, and Larry Bailey came in from Cramford. He knew my mate to say hello to. I think they used to play football in the same team when they were lads. Dimitri Spirios came from the back and saw Larry chatting to Helen, and he went ballistic. He ordered Larry outside. Dimitri called him a fat pig. At that Larry told him to stick his chips where the sun doesn't shine, then winked at Helen and left. My mate said everyone knew Larry had been seeing her for ages."

"Wow, this is interesting."

Series Three
Book Three
in the John Gammon Detective Series

"It gets better Sir, because after Larry was found murdered Helen took up with a Polish guy, Raitus Esmar, who apparently went to the same gym as Helen. They called her the Black Widow, you know after the Black Widow spider."

"Anymore Magic?"

"No, that's it Sir."

"Ok, so going back to point one. I fully understand, but you need to be patient and I will try and sort. With regard to the second point, that's great information Magic, thank you."

Magic left Gammon's office feeling quite pleased with himself.

Gammon wrote down what Magic had told him. He just needed the information about fish warehouses and the crash helmet thing from DI Bass.

BODY PARTS

He sat pondering. Could Dimitri Spirios be our killer? He ticked the boxes; worked with fish, had a temper, probably knew about his wife's dalliance with other men. Or had he just killed her? Then read about the serial killer and killed his wife in the same way so the serial killer took the blame. Either way Gammon was going to have him in once he had all the facts.

It was now almost 5.38pm and John decided he would go and see Saron. She had sounded a bit concerned. The drive from Bixton to the Tow'd Man was idyllic, the lush green fields complemented the peaks. John could see in the distance walkers heading up Barrel Peak. They looked like worker ants in the distance marching up the peak.

John had so much heartache since he come home, but that's what it really came down to the Peak District was home. He comforted himself in the fact that all the people he had lost would have left his life anyway. None of them were his fault.

The sun was just starting to go down as he pulled on the Tow'd Man car park. The sky towards Monkdale was an array of colours.

John went down the steps to enter past the kitchen thinking Saron would be working, but there was a chef chopping onions. John shouted hello and carried on into the bar. He was quite surprised to see Saron working behind the bar.

"Hey John, you ok?"

There were about ten walkers all sat in one corner, and that was it with it being early.

"What do you want to drink?"

BODY PARTS

"I'll try a pint of Swinster Swill, sounds delicious," and he laughed.

"Sold almost four barrels since Sunday, John."

"How come you are behind the bar?"

"Donna has gone to see her brother in Australia. It's a chance in a lifetime, she has gone for six weeks."

"Do you know anybody that could run the bar for me while she's away?

"Not sure, but I will have a think. So who is the chef?"

"Oh, just an agency guy, flippin driving me mad and its only day one, John."

"It's lovely to see you but it is so sad what happened to Sandra. Bet her mum and Rosie are devastated. Did you say she is selling up?"

"Yeah, Scilly Isles she said. Bit early I think, but we will see, eh."

"Are you coming to the dog races with me?"

"When's that, Saron?"

"This Saturday."

"Can you get time off?"

"Joni said she would come and cover for me. I can trust her."

"Oh, great then yeah. How do we get there?"

"Bob and Cheryl have arranged it."

"They never said the other night."

"I told them not to tell you because I wanted to treat you."

This is going well John thought as Saron headed down the bar to serve two local lads. She had a red top which hung off each shoulder showing her beautiful smooth shoulders. She had a pair of white cropped trousers and a pair of red kitten heel shoes John couldn't take his eyes off her.

BODY PARTS

"Who's going?"

"Jack and Shelley, Steve and Imogen from the Star, Kev and Doreen, Carol Lestar, Tracey Rodgers, me and you, Bob and Cheryl and I think Sheba and Phil."

"Well nobody told me anything."

"I know, I told them not to. It was a surprise for you."

"Some detective I am, Saron," and John laughed.

"Are you stopping here tonight?"

John couldn't believe his luck, everything seemed perfect.

"Well yes, if you don't mind?"

"I wouldn't have asked you if I minded."

By 10.00pm the chef had gone and all the customers in the bar had left.

"John, you lock up and I will powder my nose, then come up. There is a bottle of

Prosecco and two glasses in the fridge. Bring it up when you come up."

John thought about pinching himself it was going so well.

John went round the bar and restaurant turning lights off. Then he locked all the exterior doors, before grabbing the drink and the two glasses, and making his way up the stairs to Saron's bedroom. Saron was still in the bathroom, so John poured two glasses of Prosecco and put one on the bedside table next to Saron and one on his side. John removed his trousers and shirt just as the door opened. Saron stood in the doorway in a small purple basque with small red bows on it. Her perfectly formed bust sat perched invitingly in the basque. Her long silky legs finished off with a pair purple stiletto heeled shoes, with a small red bow on each shoe.

BODY PARTS

John grabbed her in his muscular arms, kissing first her neck, then kissing her neck and her ear lobes. Saron screamed with ecstasy, her ear lobes and neck were her weak spots.

Saron was breathless.

"I want to explore every inch of your body, my lovely."

"Do it. Do it," she said in uncontrollable words.

John gently slid his hands down Saron's milky thighs. Her head swaying from side to side in anticipation. Saron gazed into John's eyes as he kissed her.

"Tell me what you want," he said.

"You, I want you, John."

"Invite me in my lovely."

"Take me John, I am about to explode."

John lowered her onto the bed and made passionate love to the one girl he had always loved. After much energetic love making they finally lay back, both of their contentment realised.

Saron cuddled into John twirling the hairs on his chest.

"I have missed you so much, John. I hate myself for the way I shut you out because of the wedding, but you hurt me so much. I am sad we never married, but it was better than me finding out you had slept with Anouska on the eve of the wedding. I could never have forgiven you for that had we made our wedding vows."

"Are we good now?"

"I want you to promise me John, no more secrets."

At this point John had a choice, should he tell Saron about Anka Emily and risk losing her forever, or should he say nothing? The coward in John chose the

second option, tell her nothing and he just
might keep her.

They cuddled together like an old
married couple. Saron seemed content but
as usual John had fears his secret would
one day surface.

The following morning Saron was up
cooking breakfast for them both. John
showered and went downstairs. Saron
grabbed him planting a big kiss on his lips.

"Do you know what Mr Gammon, I love
you."

"I love you babe, where do we go from
here?"

Saron put the breakfast down.

"I think we should just enjoy each
other's company for a while, before we do
anything like moving in together. When
you said Lady Hasford was selling Pritwich

Hall I am guessing she will sell Sandra's cottage. I thought that would make a nice investment for me John, and if we got together permanently it would make a nice family home to bring children up in. Pritwich is a nice village, don't you think?"

"Yeah lovely, Saron."

It was clear to John that Saron had forgiven him, but this was his last chance. She was talking about a family, what if Anouska ever turned up with Anka Emily?"

"Right sweetheart, best nip home to get changed then off to work. I need to find this killer."

Saron kissed John and said to be at the Tow'd Man for 6.15pm tomorrow for the dog racing in Sheffield.

John nipped home and changed, then headed onto Bixton police station. The

BODY PARTS

information Magic had given John meant he needed to speak with Dimitri Spirios, but first it was the meeting in the incident room.

Everyone was assembled. The incident board was looking full with poor Sandra now added. First up was John Walvin.

"Yes, Wally."

"The blood splatter we found was not human."

Wally sat down.

"DS Bass, what about these helmets?"

"I went to all four suspects who all had or have had motorbikes, but none had the word IRON on the back."

"Are you sure they showed you all their hats?"

"Yes Sir, they all had at least two helmets but nothing."

Damn Gammon thought.

"Ok DI Smarty, what did your team find with regards to fish places where Sandra may have been kept?"

"We checked Hittington Fishing lake sheds, two fishing warehouses used by a local supplier to pubs that was in Cramford and five fish and chips shops at Dilley Dale, Hittington, Rowksly, Puddle Dale and Cramford. Everything came up a blank, Sir."

"Damn, right DI Milton get me Dimitri Spirios in for questioning. Tell him to bring his solicitor also. Once you have him at the station fetch me and I will interview him with you."

"Ok, thanks everybody."

Gammon went back upstairs feeling quite low. He stood looking at the fantastic view toward Losehill when Margaret Bradbury came in.

BODY PARTS

"Hi John, I have been thinking, I can't really help you much more, and there is a big case in Dorset that I have been asked to look at. Do you mind if I go back?"

"Hey, that's not a problem Margaret, the help you have given us was invaluable. You must keep in touch."

Gammon thought it was a good idea as Margaret would be a good contact for him in the future. Her line of policing was very in vogue, and an area Gammon wasn't particularly up to speed with.

At 2.30pm Milton arrived and said he was interview room two with Dimitri Spirios and his solicitor, a Mr Foley."

Gammon went down, and Milton introduced everyone for the tape.

"What is this about, Mr Gammon? I run a chip shop. I hurt nobody and my wife she now dead."

Dimitri started to cry.

"Mr Spirios, or can I call you Dimitri?"

Spirios nodded to say it was ok.

"We have concerns at this point in time. We have a credible witness who said you have a violent temper."

"I don't have a bad temper. Who says this?" Dimitri asked in his Derbyshire /Greek brogue.

"I am not at liberty to say, Dimitri. My source tells me you also had a big fall out with one of the victims a Larry Bailey."

Dimitri at this point lost his self-control and punched the table. His solicitor tried to calm him down.

"That low life snake. He try it on with my wife. How would you a feel? It is a not fair, I am honest hard-working man. I do nothing to him."

"That is not what I am told, Dimitri. Dimitri, I am going to ask you a couple of questions, think very hard before you answer. Did you kill Larry Bailey?"

"What, is this some kind of bloody stitch up?" he said flailing his arms about vigorously.

"So, is that yes or no?"

"It's a bloody no."

The solicitor kept trying to calm him down.

"Did you kill your wife Dimitri?"

"You bloody copper, I told you I do nothing."

"What about DI Scooper, who incidentally had been held hostage somewhere where fish were stored? You have fish, don't you Dimitri?"

"You go to hell, you bloody thing," he swore.

"How well did you know Alan Hewitt?"

"I don't know Alan Hewitt."

"What about DCI Saul Dirk?"

"Mr Dirk, he come to my shop to buy fish and chips for him and his wife."

"So, you knew DCI Dirk then?"

"I told you he good customer."

"Ok Dimitri, what about Raitus Esmar?"

"He was piece of shit. He always come in my shop and say rude things to my wife. I didn't like him."

Gammon looked at Milton. They were both thinking this could be their killer.

"We believe you have a motorbike?"

"Yes, I did, but I no ride anymore. I told your young police woman that."

I take it that was DS Bass?"

"Yes, DS Bass, why you ask me again?"

BODY PARTS

"It's all part of our investigation, Dimitri. Your wife Helen, would you say you had a loving relationship?"

"She was my wife!"

"I know that, but would you say you were complete as a couple?"

"We work together and build business. We do good she want for nothing."

"Did you have any marital problems? I see you didn't have children?"

"My wife, she a hot blooded Greek woman. She want baby, but I have problem so we no have babies."

"This is a hard question to ask you, but I'm afraid it has to be asked. Did your wife have affairs during your marriage?"

"Why you bloody ask me this, people been bloody talking?"

"Our source tells us she had at least two extra marital affairs; one with Alan Hewitt who is now deceased, and one with Raitus Esmar. Were you aware of these Dimitri?"

Dimitri was quite calm, and he leaned towards his solicitor and whispered something,

"Yes, I know these men they try to take my Helen from me, and a bloody copper as well."

"A copper, who might that be?"

"She told me his name was Dirk."

"Dirk Saul?"

"Yes, that was his name. I told him not to come to my chip shop again, copper or no copper."

Gammon looked at Milton.

"Dimitri Spirios, I am going to hold you for fourty eight hours. In that time a full search of your home your business and vehicles will be carries out. Do you have any land that we need to be aware of?"

BODY PARTS

"I have two acres on Micklock Moor, with a horse for my wife on it."

"Are there any buildings on this land?"

"Yes of course, a stable and tack room."

"Ok, DI Milton will take you to the holding cell. Depending on what we find we will then decide if you will be charged with any of the murders we are investigating."

Dimitri became upset.

"What about my shop? People come for miles on Friday for my fish supper."

"Well I am afraid they will be disappointed tonight, Dimitri. Take Mr Spirios down to the holding cells please DI Milton."

Gammon turned to the solicitor.

"I would like to see you and your client at 10.00am on Monday."

Gammon felt they had their man. His instinct told him that Spirios killed the men who and affair with his wife, including DCI Dirk, but he didn't get the Sandra murder. Why was she killed, or did he not kill Sandra?

It was now almost 5.00pm and Gammon had arranged for Wally and his team plus all his detectives to meet at the Rowksly chip shop at 9.00am. the next morning. He told Smarty that once they had done what they could they would move up to Micklock Moor and the stables and tack room. He had just 48 hours to either charge or let Spirios go. So everybody was told they had to be in at the weekend.

Gammon left Bixton and headed to see Kev. On the way he rang Saron to say he was working the weekend, but he would be at the Tow'd Man in time for the bus to the races.

He had almost arrived at the Spinning Jenny when his phone rang. It was Lady Hasford. She said Sandra's funeral would be at St Matthew's Church in Alstongate, a village close to Pritwich. Sandra had sung in the choir as a little girl and Lady Hasford and her husband paid for a new church roof nine years previously.

Lady Hasford asked if he would do a eulogy. Chief Constable Sim had asked if it was ok for her colleagues to carry the coffin into and to the grave, as she wanted to be buried.

"Lady Hasford, I would be honoured to deliver a eulogy and I know her colleagues would want to carry her coffin."

"Ok, thank you John. The funeral will be on Tuesday at 11.00am at St Matthews

Church in Alstongate, and everyone is welcome back at The Wobbly Man in Toad Holes for food and drinks after the burial."

"Ok, I will tell everyone. Is there anything you or Rosie need me to do for you?"

"No, we are fine John, but thank you for the offer," and Lady Hasford ended the call saying goodbye as she broke down on the phone.

This must be so hard for her and Rosie John thought. There was one thing for sure, he would not let this rest until her killer was arrested.

He arrived at the Spinning Jenny and told Kev about the arrangements for Sandra's funeral.

"Very sad lad, very sad, and now that little girl has no mum or dad. I hope whoever did this rots in hell."

BODY PARTS

"I hope I'm not the arresting officer Kev, or I probably won't be responsible for my actions."

"I know what you mean. Listen mate I'll just have a quick pint, and would Doreen do me a take out?"

"What do you fancy, lad?"

Kev gave him a menu.

"I like the look of that."

John pointed at the cubed sirloin steak, marinated in red wine, shallots and cream with black pudding mash with hint of horseradish and country vegetables.

"Doreen came up with this about five weeks ago and we sell out every week, John."

"Right mate, I'm going for that."

John managed two pints before his dinner came through, and headed home with full intention of writing Sandra's eulogy.

He had just poured himself a drink and took his first mouthful of food when his phone rang. It was Chief Constable Sim.

"Good evening John, with the current situation at Bixton, and this is not a reflection of you, Sir Gavin Boomer informed me that DI Danny Kiernan will be coming to help out at Bixton until we get a break through on the cases. Look on it as a bonus John. DI Kiernan has a wealth of experience with these sort of cases, and it's rare you get help from Scotland Yard. Can you pick him up from Bixton station at 8.00am and find him somewhere to stay until it's all sorted?"

"Ok Sir, will do."

"Thanks John, speak soon," and Sim hung up.

BODY PARTS

Bloody hell Gammon thought that's two bloody rookies to sort; DS John Winnipeg and now flippin' Detective Inspector Danny Kiernan from Scotland Yard, whoever he is?

John finished his tea and made a start on Sandra's eulogy. It was gone 1.00am by the time he was happy with what he had written, so he headed for bed.

CHAPTER SEVEN

The following morning John rang Lisa
Tink to see if she could put up Danny
Kiernan. Lisa said there wasn't a problem,
so they arranged that Kiernan would be
dropping his things off around 8.30am.

Gammon showered then headed for
Bixton train station to meet DI Kiernan.
The train was half empty as it pulled into
Bixton. The tall well-dressed, good looking
guy stood out like a sore thumb from the
rest of the passengers.

Gammon wandered over. He could see
Kiernan had a few designer labels on which
reminded him of himself when he first
came to Derbyshire from Scotland Yard.

Gammon thrust out his hand.

"Daniel Kiernan?"

The guy looked startled.

BODY PARTS

"DCI John Gammon, Buxton police."

"Oh, nice to meet you, Sir."

"Likewise, now is it Daniel or Danny?"

"I don't have a preference, Sir. My mum calls me Daniel but most of my friends call me Danny."

"Ok, then Danny it is. Did you have a good journey?"

"Yes Sir, early start though. "

"My senior officer said you worked in Scotland Yard.

"He said to send his best wishes."

"Who was that?"

"DCI Chris Ingo."

"Bloody hell, not bloody Bingo?"

"Yes, they do call him that, but not to his face, Sir. Why do they call him Bingo?"

"Well, his full name is Robert Christopher Ingo, but he uses his middle name because if he wrote Bob Ingo as just B Ingo, it's "BINGO"."

Once he had composed himself Danny apologised.

"No skin off my nose lad, I always thought it was funny anyway. So old Bingo made DCI, did he?"

"Yes Sir, about four years back."

"Oh well, good luck to him, he was basically a nice guy."

"I have you booked in at a nice place in a little village called Clough Dale. It's run by a very nice couple, Lisa and Jim Tink."

Lisa met them, and Danny dropped his things off.

They went to Spirios's chip shop and Gammon called an introduction meeting.

"I would like Smarty, Milton, Lee, Magic to meet our two new recruits; DI

BODY PARTS

Danny Kiernan from Scotland Yard and the one we thought we would never see, DS John Winnipeg."

Winnipeg stood up. He was a tall guy very confident with a great smile.

"I'm sure you will give them as much help as they need. Remember everyone we are searching the chip shop for any signs that Sandra may have been held there or any of our victims. Then there is land at Micklock with stables on it that Spirios owns. We will move to that once a comprehensive search has been carried out here."

"DI Milton, fill DS Winnipeg and DI Kiernan in on the cases, victims, suspects etc. You will need to run DI Kiernan about until he returns to London."

"DS Winnipeg, where are you staying?"

Series Three
Book Three
in the John Gammon Detective Series

"My girlfriend has got a job at Bixton General, so we have rented a house in Pritwich until we get settled."

"Ok, so you are sorted then."

"Carl it's just Danny to look after. He is staying at Jim and Lisa Tink's place, Cambridge Lodge in Clough Dale."

"Ok, Sir."

Wally and his team had been there an hour. He was always afraid of people contaminating a possible crime scene before he had time to gather evidence.

"Morning Wally."

"Good Morning, John."

"Poor morning, not sure this mist is going to lift today."

"Yes, not good Wally, you just setting up?

BODY PARTS

"Yes, we are going to do the store shed first."

The store shed was in what had been a back garden before the old house had become a chip shop. It was quite well cared for. The woodwork was painted green and it had a big padlock on the door, which two PC's broke off for Wally.

"I'll let you crack on Wally, my team will help you."

"That's what I am frightened of John," and he smiled as he ducked under the tent entrance covering the door to the store shed.

"Sir, come round here."

"What is it, DI Lee?"

"This lock has been forced, somebody has been in here I think."

Series Three
Book Three
in the John Gammon Detective Series

"Well there isn't much damage to the lock. Get Wally to send somebody over to look at it."

The team went through everything, but found nothing. Wally said he wouldn't know his results until 9.00 am Monday.

It was almost 1.00pm as they headed for the stables at Micklock. Gammon was mindful he had promised Saron he would be at the Tow'd Man at 6.15 pm for the mini bus to the dogs.

Micklock Moor was like a scene from Wuthering Heights. The mist swirled round the desolate moorland as they arrived at the stables.

One team got to work in the stable blocks and another team in the big shed. They had been searching for about an hour when Di Kiernan shouted Gammon across.

"Found this, Sir."

BODY PARTS

Danny Kiernan showed Gammon a Blue John chain and pendent. Gammon knew immediately that it was Sandra's because he bought it her many years before. They bagged it up for Wally. It was now almost 4.00pm and they had about done.

"Ok everyone, thanks for giving up your weekend but hopefully Wally will have something for us Monday morning."

John arrived back and quickly showered and changed into his clothes for the night out with Saron.

It was just gone 6.15pm, so he got some stick as he got on the minibus with Bob leading a chorus song of 'Why Are We Waiting'. Cheryl was doing her obligatory hand waving at Bob telling him to stop it.

"Thought you were going to let me down, John."

"Never, you look stunning, Saron."

She had a tight fitting dark blue dress with a cream shawl and cream Jimmy Choo shoes.

"Thank you, kind Sir. You don't look bad yourself," she laughed while she pecked him on the cheek.

Bob stood up.

"Listen everyone, here are your tickets. We are in the posh end and you get a three-course meal which you have all ordered."

"Don't worry John, already done yours."

"Oh, good."

"Just show your ticket at the door and they will show us to our table."

The Greyhound stadium had been upgraded from the last time John had been some twenty years before. They had a great table overlooking the track. Saron had ordered the same as her for dinner; Thai

BODY PARTS

fishcakes to start, sirloin steak chips and veg and a chocolate melt in the middle pudding with cream.

"Blimey Saron, for what we paid that was excellent. I'll nip and get us a drink."

"You don't have to John, they will bring them to you and take your bets."

"This is the life Bob, I could get used to this."

Kev shouted from further down the table.

"You would not get this in The Spinning Jenny lad."

"He already bloody does, Kevin."

"Yeah, you spoil him, Doreen."

"Certainly do Shelley, don't I sweetheart?"

"Yes Doreen, thank you."

With the meal polished off it was time for the racing. John put ten pounds win on Nightingale Lass and Saron did ten pounds on Sovereign Lassy. While they were waiting for the dogs they split the table into one and two with six people on each. Bob said to watch the dogs as they do a small circuit in a paddock and invariably they go to the toilet. Everyone on each table had to put a pound each on the dog number they thought would go to the toilet first.

"Bob, this sounds a bit crude."

"I promise you Shelley, you will have a right laugh."

By the end of the night the excitement was more on the dump competition than the actual races. John was thirty five pounds up, Kev was seventy seven pounds up and Jack was fifteen pounds up. The rest all lost, even though Doreen won the most dumps competition, winning twenty five pounds.

BODY PARTS

They arrived back at the Tow'd Man, dropping John and Saron off. Then the bus took the rest to the Spinning Jenny to be dropped off.

"That was a real laugh John, wasn't it?"

"Yeah, and only Bob could come up with a dog dump competition!"

Saron poured them both a drink and they headed to bed. Within minutes of lying on John's chest she was asleep. John lay looking out at the stars. He couldn't believe he was in the arms of Saron. He never thought that she would ever forgive him, but she had, and it was up to him to make sure he gave her his trust back.

In the morning John said he would call Saron later, he wanted to go back to his place and put the final touches to Sandra's eulogy.

As John sat writing he smiled to himself at some of the things they had gotten up to, and how she was always supportive of John at all times. He remembered something Annie Tanney said to him not long before she died.

"Remember John, small memories will one day be big memories. Those you love and lose will always remember those memories even in their afterlife because memories are made together."

Before he knew it Monday morning had come round and he had everyone assembled in the incident room. This was decision day with Spirios.

"Good morning everyone. As you know we have until lunchtime to either charge this man," and Gammon pointed to a picture of Dimitri Spirios. "Or let him go. Wally we are relying on you."

John Walvin came to the front.

"Right, well first of all, the chip shop in Rowksly, we found nothing untoward in the actual chip shop but the door at the rear of the property had been forced off that there is no doubt."

"Now on Micklock Moor the pendent found by DI Kiernan was definitely DI Scooper's. There was her DNA all over it. We found no trace of any of the suspects' DNA in the shed or on anything including the pendent. We are quite sure that Sandra had been there at some time, but when and for how long I can't say."

"Ok, thanks to you and your team for working over the weekend."

"Yes, DI Kiernan?"

"Sir, I came in with DI Milton on Sunday and ran a check on Mr Spirios and his accounts. He has three accounts; a business accounts with Lloyds which appears to be all above board. Then there was a joint account between him and his wife, the deceased Helen. This appears to be mainly used by Helen for food shopping, fuel and clothes. It was the last account which was just in the name of Dimitri Spirios. This account had payments to Lund Enterprises. They were quite substantial, there was a monthly one on the third of every month for six hundred pounds and invariably there would also be five or six payments of around eighty pounds most weeks."

"Thank you DI Kiernan, good work."

The new man positively beamed as he sat down.

BODY PARTS

"Ok, I want Milton and Smarty to accompany me. Is Spirios's lawyer here?"

"Yes, been here since 9.00am, Sir. He's keen to get his client off."

"Well we will see about that. Let's go and ask more questions, shall we?"

With that the meeting broke up and Gammon, Milton and Smarty headed for the interview room.

Milton set the tape up and Gammon started questioning Dimitri.

His opening line was, "I never hurt nobody Mr Gammon. I love my wife."

"Mr Spirios, we have done a thorough search of your house and sheds on Micklock Moor, and I would like clarification with what we found. At the chip shop in Rowksly the rear door had been forced. Was that of your doing?"

"No, it will be robbers."

"So, you think somebody broke into your shop and home?"

"Yes, must be because I not there."

"Well let me tell you nothing looked disturbed. If that is the case, what were they looking for?"

"I don't know."

"You see Mr Spirios, I think you do know, don't you?"

"No, you bloody copper, I don't."

"Ok, let's move our attention to the stables and shed on Micklock Moor, where we found this."

Gammon showed Spirios the Blue John pendent.

"What is this?"

"It's DI Scooper's pendent which was found in your shed on the moor."

"I never see this before."

BODY PARTS

"Again Mr Spirios, I think you are lying."

"You all bloody bent coppers," he said banging his fist on the table.

"Now your bank accounts, of which we found three. One a business account, two is a joint account with your deceased wife, Helen. Now the really interesting account is number three. Who are Lund Enterprises, Mr Spirios?"

Spirios whispered in the ear of his solicitor.

"I can't tell you, Mr Gammon."

"Well, I would just take a minute, because if I don't get straight answers then I will be charging you."

Again, Spirios spoke with his solicitor.

"Look Mr Gammon, I tell you then I am dead man walking."

"If you don't, you are dead man talking."

"Mr Gammon, I do nothing wrong, please don't make me say."

"Speak now Dimitri, or take the consequences."

"Ok, two years ago my brother he come to live with me and Helen for two years. While he is here he goes to Derby to meet ladies. Anyway, one night he come home, and his arm is burnt. He say men want money of him, and when he don't give them money they scalded him. I very angry. My little brother, they can't do this to him, so I go find these men and I take baseball bat."

Gammon instinctively knew that this was all to do with Brian Lund. But now he was dead he would possibly not be able to do anything.

"I find these men in pub, Drovers Arms in Derby. I ask who do this to my baby brother? A big fat man he said I do, what I am going to do? I pull the baseball bat from under my coat. I say I hit you with this. He laughed at me and four big men jumped on me and hit me very hard. Then I get taken to a room where I am told that from now on the third of every month I pay Lund Enterprises for protection."

"What is your brother's name, Dimitri?"

"Aldis Spirios."

"Where is Aldis now, so that we can verify his version of events?"

Dimitri leaned forward and whispered in his solicitor's ear. There was a pause before he answered.

"I don't know, he go."

"Go where, Dimitri?"

"I tell you, I don't know."

"Is he still in the UK?"

"I don't know, I don't care," he said, and he stood up waving his fists.

His solicitor got him to sit down.

"You have a violent temper there, Dimitri. I suspect that you killed these people we are investigating, and possibly your wife and your brother, am I correct?"

"No, I loved my wife. He was treacherous."

"Explain, Dimitri."

"I find him in my bed with Helen, and we fight. That's why he leave."

"Is that why you killed your wife?"

"I bloody told you, I no kill my wife."

"Let's go back to DI Scooper's pendent. Why would that be found on a property you own?"

"I tell you, I don't know reason."

Gammon told Milton to pause the tape and he asked DI Smarty to step outside.

BODY PARTS

"What do you think, Dave?"

"Everything points to him. He appears to have a fiery temper and his missus played around. It would be very coincidental if he wasn't involved, and with Sandra's pendent found at one of his sheds on Micklock Moor, it certainly makes him the prime suspect, I think."

"I'm not sure there is enough to convict him, Dave. Last thing I need is a wrong decision, now I have this post, that's why I asked you for your opinion.

Think you are right. If we charge him and it's wrong all damnation will fall on Bixton. Now you are heading it up it, wouldn't be good for you John."

"Ok, let's go back in."

Gammon indicated to Milton to start the tape running.

Series Three
Book Three
in the John Gammon Detective Series

"Dimitri Spirios, we have taken the decision to release you without charge at this present time, while we try and locate your brother. I no doubt will need you to attend for further questioning while the case is on-going. You are free to go."

Spirios pulled a handkerchief from his pocket and dabbed each eye. He was certainly relieved as he left the room and the station with his freedom, albeit not for long Gammon thought.

On the way out Gammon tasked DI Milton with finding Aldis Spirios.

Two days passed and things in John's social life were very good. Saron was taking time from the pub and it really looked like they would try to work things out. The case hadn't gone much further.

BODY PARTS

Aldis Spirios appeared to have disappeared off the face of the earth.

Saron had arranged with John to have a meal at the Spinning Jenny. She had had seen a critics review in the Derbyshire Country Life. John was happy with that. He liked the Spinning Jenny and he could have a drink with Kev after the meal. Little was John to know what lay ahead.

They arrived for the meal and Doreen showed them into the restaurant.

"Hope you like our new menu. A critic from Derbyshire Country Life gave it five stars."

"Yes, I know Doreen, that's why I suggest we booked a table."

"Well its lovely to see you, and lovely to see you together. Here are the menus. What would you like to drink?"

Series Three
Book Three
in the John Gammon Detective Series

"Let's have a bottle of champagne, Saron."

"Sounds good to me."

"Champagne it is then," and Doreen left them musing over the menu.

"Sorry John, I am going to have to nip to the ladies room."

"No problem sweetheart, there is no rush, we have all night."

Saron left John deciding what to order. Three or four minutes passed and no sign of Doreen with the champagne or Saron. It was almost fifteen minutes gone when Doreen arrived.

"I am guessing you don't want this now?"

"Yes of course, I was just going to ask you to check on Saron. She went to the ladies room."

BODY PARTS

"She didn't get there, John. I'm afraid Anouska is in the bar with a baby."

"What, you are joking. So where is Saron?"

"She ran outside crying, so I followed her to ask what was the matter. She said about you sleeping with Anouska on your wedding night. To compound it she said Anouska has a baby which she has called Anka Emily. I think she put two and two together with Emily being your mother's name."

"I best go after her."

"No you don't. She is livid with you. She said to tell you not to follow her, she was really upset, John."

"But I need to explain to her Doreen. I can't leave it like this."

Doreen sat at the table and poured a glass of champagne for them both.

"Right lad, its cards on the table time. Is that little one yours?"

John coloured up.

"I am guessing by the silence that's a yes then. I am also guessing you haven't told Saron."

"Doreen, how could I?"

"Well for a bloody good copper, you can be stupid at times, John."

"Look, I wish it never happened but it did. Me and Saron were starting to work things out. There was no way I could tell her, Doreen."

"So, have you seen the baby?"

"No, I haven't."

"Well now is the time, she is in the bar, brazen as ever."

John's heart was thumping as he left the restaurant and headed for the bar to see Anouska and the baby. When he got there, she had gone. Kev came from out of the back room.

"You ok lad? You look like you have seen a ghost."

John ordered two double brandies; one for him and one for Kev and he started to tell him what had happened.

"Bloody hell John, you have made a right mess of this. Is there any wonder she ran out?"

"So now what are you going to do?"

"I really don't know. She told Doreen that I wasn't to contact her."

"Who, Anouska?"

"No, Saron. I don't know where Anouska and the baby have gone, Kev. This has turned out to be a disaster, Kev. It always seems to happen to me!"

"I think you need to take a long hard look at yourself mate."

**Series Three
Book Three
in the John Gammon Detective Series**

By all most 10.30pm they were both well on their way. Doreen had told Kev to lock up at 11.00pm. She had breakfast to do the following day, so she was calling it a night. It was 10.45pm and there was just Kev and John sat determined to finish the bottle, when Anouska walked back in, but on her own.

Kev left them to it and went to cash up.

"Why are you back, Anouska? You said you wouldn't be."

"Do you not want to see your baby, John?"

"I told you I am trying to make a go with Saron, and now seeing you has blown it."

"John, come with me. I want you to see our baby girl."

"Where is she?"

"She is with a friend in Bixton, please you come."

BODY PARTS

John was at that stage after drinking when sense wasn't something he could do, so he left with Anouska.

"Wow, I like the car."

"It's my friend's. She let me borrow it."

Anouska and John arrived at what had been originally council flats, but people had been allowed to buy them, so they weren't too bad.

Anouska opened the door and a woman in her mid-forties said hello. Anouska introduced John. The woman then left the room. Anouska became all attentive and John's defence wasn't good because of the brandy. She slipped off her coat and sensually played her hands up and down John. John remembered how weak he had been the last time, and it was shaping up to be like that now. Within minutes they were making love. Well, it wasn't love, it was lust. Not many men would have been able to say no to Anouska John thought.

After it was over John asked about Anka. She is asleep. You can see her in the morning. You need sleep because you drink too much."

John was soon fast asleep.

The following morning he woke with a start and the feeling of not really knowing where he was. He sat for a few minutes gathering his thoughts. The flat seemed eerily quiet. John decided to try and find Anouska and the baby, but all the rooms were empty. There was nothing.

John didn't know what was going on, but he did know he needed to get out. He had only just got on the stairwell when a young couple went to the flat. John watched as the guy opened the door. The woman screamed, "Where's our furniture?"

BODY PARTS

John, a DCI, could not be seen here. So he scuttled away as quick as his legs could carry him.

It was now the day of Sandra's funeral, something he had been dreading. He had tried for three or four days to speak with Saron, but she didn't want to speak with him.

The officers from the station that were carrying the coffin had been sent to Lady Hasford. John headed straight to Matthews Church at Alstongate. The weather was typical funeral weather; damp, drizzly and overcast. The old Saxon church wasn't big, so he thought there would be few people outside. John wasn't wrong. The church was full, only the saved family pews and the police pews were vacant.

Sandra's coffin was brought into one of her favourite songs 'What's Going On' by Marvin Gaye. She had often played this to John and he could feel the emotion welling up inside him.

The Bixton police team carried in the coffin and placed it in front of the small altar. It had a spray of white and pink lilies with Sandra's police hat in the centre. John could hear the congregation getting upset as the vicar Reverend Lowe climbed the steps of the pulpit.

"I hope all here today will join with me in celebrating the life of Sandra Francesca Olivier Scooper, a colleague to some and a friend to all of you. Sandra was taken from us all too early, but it is my belief her life has only just begun, as she takes her journey onto everlasting life."

BODY PARTS

"Sandra, as a young girl, sang in the choir here at St Matthews so many of you parishioners will have known Sandra well. Sandra was well liked by everyone she met. She always had time to care, not only in her role as a police officer, but in her private life."

"I would like you to stand for our first hymn 'How Great Thou Art'. The congregation sang loudly. Chief Inspector Sim had a very good voice and his voice led the way.

At the end the vicar said that Chief Constable Andrew Sim from Derbyshire Police would like to say a few words and that Detective Inspector John Gammon would do an eulogy.

John looked across and Lady Hasford who was sobbing with little Rosie looking at her in bewilderment.

Sim started his address.

"I knew of Detective Inspector Scooper, although I didn't know her personally, so that side I will leave to my colleague John."

"What I can tell you is Sandra Scooper was an excellent officer. She had guile, guts and a strong sense of doing things right. Derbyshire and the Peak District owe Sandra a great debt of gratitude with her dedication to keeping our communities safe."

"If there is a police force up there, then they are getting one hell of a police officer," and Sim then gestured to John to take over.

John cleared his throat and started.

"I first met Sandra on my return to Bixton, which is now a good few years ago. I remember one of our first conversations

BODY PARTS

when I suggested I would understand, with Rosie only being small, that she possibly could not put the hours in that the other officers could. Well let me tell you, that was my first mistake. Sandra was having none of it. If anything, it spurred her on to prove me wrong, which she certainly did."

"Sandra would often bring a coffee into my office when she had found some information she had been working on. I can see her now placing the plastic cup on a coaster she bought me, because she said I would ruin my desk drinking the dishwater, as I called it."

"Sandra was a good friend to me when I lost my brother, then my father and mother. She was always there when I had a low moment. The job we do requires concentration, compassion, dedication and the ability to put others first. Sandra

Scooper had all these attributes and more. I would just like to read a verse that really sums my friend and colleague Detective Inspector Sandra Scooper."

"When I come to the end of the road
and the sun has set for me
I want no rites in a gloom filled room
Why cry for a soul set free?
Miss me a little, but not for long
and not with your head bowed low
Remember the fun that once we shared
Miss me, but let me go.
For this is a journey we all must take
and each must go alone.
It's all part of the master plan
a step on the road to home.
When you are lonely and sick at heart
go to the friends we know.
Laugh at all the things we used to done

BODY PARTS

Go now on your journey. Goodbye and God bless you, Sandra Scooper."

John wiped a small tear from his eye and left the pulpit to take his place next to Lady Hasford and little Rosie.

The vicar stood in the pulpit.

"Take joy, brothers and sisters, for the life Sandra. We all have tribulations in our lives, these are tests of your faith which gives us perseverance. Let perseverance finish its work so that you may be mature and complete, not lacking anything."

"Lady Hasford has asked that you join her and Rosie at The Wobbly Man in Toad Holes for light refreshments."

"If the congregation would please stand for our final hymn 'Lord of all hopefulness'."

There was not a dry eye in the church while the hymn was being sung. Sandra's colleagues lifted the coffin from in front of the alter. Everyone had tears rolling down their faces as they proceeded to leave the church to the Eva Cassidy song 'Somewhere over the Rainbow'. Close family, John and Andrew Sim went to the graveside.

As they lowered the coffin Lady Hasford put her arm on John's shoulder and simply said, "Thank you."

Back at the Wobbly Man, Carl Milton told Dave Smarty that there must have been over eighty mourners that had come back. Smarty had got John a drink when John spied Saron in the corner speaking with John Walvin. She looked like a movie star in a little black dress, complemented with a

pearl necklace and black shoes and
handbag. John thought about going over,
but didn't want any unpleasantness. He had
enough for one day he thought.

Lord and Lady Cote-Heath arranged to
take Lady Hasford and Rosie home. Before
she left Lady Hasford told John she had
sold Pritwich Hall to a young couple who
would be moving in four weeks. John was
shocked and was sure she was moving in
haste, but it wasn't his problem. He wanted
the person who created this carnage.

It was almost 11.00pm when John and
Dave Smarty left the Wobbly Man, both
adamant that they would get who was
responsible for the death of their friend.

The following day Gammon arrived at
Bixton.

"Good morning, Magic."

"Good morning Sir. DI Danny Kiernan wanted to see you when you got in."

"Oh ok. tell him to pop into my office please."

"Will do, Sir."

Danny Kiernan knocked on John's door.

"Come in."

"Good morning, Sir."

"Everything ok, Danny?"

"Yes, great Sir. I took a phone call about a half hour ago from an Alice Roome. She said she saw who took Sandra."

"Did you ask her to come to the station?"

"I'm afraid she isn't well enough, so I said I would go and take her statement."

"Brilliant, where does she live, Danny?"

"The old peoples' bungalows in Alford in the Water. Number seven, Sir."

"Right get DS Bass and let's go and talk to this lady."

BODY PARTS

They arrived at Alice Roome's bungalow which was directly across from where Scooper had been abducted. Alice opened her door and they showed their warrant cards.

"Do come in," she said. "Would you like a nice pot of tea and some cake perhaps?"

"No, we are fine. May I call you Alice?"

"Of course you can, Mr Gammon."

"So Alice, you spoke with DI Kiernan and you said you had information, is that correct?"

"Yes, I saw the man arguing with that police lady. I didn't know who she was until I read the article in the Micklock Mercury about her funeral, poor gal."

"So, do you know the man?"

"Well, it was a dreadful night, but his van had a lamp on top. When I told my friend next door he said they use it to hunt rabbits at night."

"What colour was the van, Alice?"

"I think it was green, but my eyes aren't what they should be, and it was a terrible night."

"So, you don't think you could give a description of the man?"

"No, he had a hat on and dark clothes, but his jacket said something on the back."

"What did it say, Alice?"

"I think the big lettering said Ackbourne, but I can't be sure. I'm not being a lot of help, am I Mr Gammon?"

"You have been, and thank you for calling us."

They went back to the car and Alice waved them off.

"Not sure we got anything from that."

BODY PARTS

"I did, Sir. When I went to check the motorbikes out, Pedro Kuna had a dark jacket on at work. In big letters it said Ackbourne then below it said Sterling's Meat Warehouse."

"That's good, but almost three hundred people work there, and they will all have the same jackets. Also Toby Glew works there."

"Ok, drop me at the station and you and DS Bass bring in Pedro Kuna. Also make sure he has a solicitor."

"Will do, Sir."

By 3.00pm Kuna and his solicitor were in the interview room with Gammon, Kiernan and DS Bass were doing the recording.

"Ok Mr Kuna, where are you from?"

"Bulgaria."

"You work at Sterling's Meat warehouse, is that correct?"

"Yes."

"So, you know Toby Glew."

"Yes, we work same shift."

"Where do you live, Mr Kuna?"

"In Rowksly."

"Can we be more specific?"

"I live in small house in village."

"Do you own the house?"

"No."

"Who does own the house?"

"Mr Spirios."

"Spirios who owns the chip shop?"

"Yes."

"Do you own a green van?"

"No."

"Do you own a van?"

"Yes, but it is grey."

BODY PARTS

"Just pause the tape, DS Bass please," and Gammon gestured DI Kiernan to follow him.

"I think we have Sandra's abductor. Get DI Smart to get a search warrant for his house. Also confiscate his van and let's get that checked over."

"Will do, Sir."

Gammon went back in the room and told Kuna he was holding him for a further 48 hours whilst they searched his house and car.

"What are you holding him on, DCI Gammon?"

"Abduction, false imprisonment and the murder of Detective Inspector Sandra Scooper."

"DS Bass, take him to the holding cells."

This wouldn't bring Sandra back, but he was hoping he had her killer.

"Well done DS Bass, good police work."
Katy beamed at Gammon's comments.

"Kate, look on Interpol to see if this guy is who he says he is, and let's see if there are any warrants out for him in Bulgaria."

"Will do, Sir."

The following morning Gammon met the team at Fisherman's cottage in Rowksly. Officers broke the door down. Gammon was first in. Nothing looked too out of place until they went up-stairs. In the first bedroom Gammon found a hand-written list of names. Against each name it noted which body part had been taken. Gammon turned to DI Lee.

"Think we might have our man, Peter. Only thing bothering me is why would he cut off body parts? It's not for trophies, surely if it is it's a bit over the top from the usual lock of hair."

They headed back to the station pleased they may have their man. A lot now hung on Wally's results from the house and Kuna's van.

Gammon sat with the note which was meticulously written but again there was something else bothering him. Something wasn't adding up.

The contents of the list began with

Alan Hewitt: Big head!! Left arm nice earner

Larry Bailey: Both legs to add to collection

Saul Dirk: Policeman thought he was that clever right arm to add to collection.

Raitus Esmar: Paid well for this one. Torso added to collection.

Series Three
Book Three
in the John Gammon Detective Series

There was no Helen Spirios or Sandra Scooper on the list. Why, he thought?

The following day they met in the incident room.

"Ok everyone, we could be on to something finally. What did you find at the house Wally?"

John Walvin came to the front.

"There was no evidence to suggest any of the victims had been to the house, but in the shed we did find a battery powered circular saw and this had Alan Hewitt's and DCI Dirk's blood on it. Other than that, nothing. We then spent time with the van. We did find DNA from Alan Hewitt, Larry Bailey, DCI Dirk and Raitus Esmar."

"What about Helen Spirios or Sandra?"

"Nothing, Sir."

"Could you be mistaken, Wally?"

BODY PARTS

Wally scowled at Gammon.

"I would say not," came his reply.

"Ok, thanks for that. So, we either have a very clever Bulgarian, either that or he wasn't working alone hence the comment of paid well. Does the fact that Helen Spirios or Sandra weren't on the list mean that they may have been murdered by a copycat killer?"

"DS Bass, Di Kiernan and DI Smarty get Kuna and his solicitor in the interview room and be prepared for a late night.

Once assembled Gammon made his way to interview room one.

"Mr Kuna, I would like you write down your address."

Kuna did as he was told. Gammon knew straight away that the list at the house wasn't his writing.

Gammon pushed the note with the killings on across to Kuna and his solicitor.

"Is this your writing?"

Kuna replied, "No comment."

He then showed Kuna the circular saw.

"Is this your saw, Mr Kuna?"

Kuna said it was much to Gammons surprise.

"Our forensic team found blood from two of the victims on this saw, Mr Kuna."

Kuna looked bemused.

"I never use saw, only once some years ago."

Gammon could feel doubts creeping in with his officers, but he ploughed on.

"We have looked at your van, and have found DNA from four victims. Can you explain that to me?"

"Again Kuna replied, "No comment."

"Did you know Helen Spirios?"

BODY PARTS

"Yes, pretty lady. She sometimes called for my rent. She is wife of Dimitri, my landlord."

"What about DI Scooper?"

"No, don't know a Scooper lady."

"Why would a note be in your bedroom stating the killings?"

"I don't know."

"Look Pedro, you are trying my patience, I want the truth."

Just then Carl Milton opened the door and gestured to Gammon to come outside.

"Pause the tape please, DS Bass."

"What is it, Carl?"

"Pedro Kuna is actually Ugis Bravas. He is on Interpol's wanted list for two murders thirteen years ago in Varna a seaside city in Bulgaria."

"Brilliant Carl," and Gammon went back in and gestured to DS Bass to start the tape.

Series Three
Book Three
in the John Gammon Detective Series

"So, Pedro Kuna or should I call you Ugis Bravas, the man wanted for two murders thirteen years ago?"

At this Pedro broke down.

"Look I do these things for somebody who said they would go to police and have me deported if I didn't."

"I'm all ears, Ugis."

"I got into a fight in a bar and a man pulled a knife on me. We wrestled, and the knife went in him. So then his friend came at me with a broken bottle and I just swung out. They both in a pool of blood so I run away because it look bad. I knew somebody who was working illegally in toy factory, so he got me job and papers."

"Where was the Toy factory?"

"It was in Dilley Dale. My friend he died one year later so John Glew he pay for funeral. I told him I was illegal immigrant.

BODY PARTS

He said my story was safe with him, but I owed him. It was John Glew who wrote the list and gave it to me."

"If I am hearing you correctly, you are saying John Glew blackmailed you to chop these people up?"

"Yes, he did. I know it wrong but he give me no choice."

"Where did he take the body parts?"

"I don't know he just collects them."

"Ugis Bravas, I am arresting you for the murders of Alan Hewitt, Larry Bailey, Saul Dirk and Raitus Esmar. You don't have to say anything..." and Gammon carried on with the arrest statement.

"DI Kiernan, take him back to the cells."

"DS Bass take DI Smarty and DS Winnipeg and arrest John Glew."

Gammon went to his office and phoned Chief Constable Sim.

Series Three
Book Three
in the John Gammon Detective Series

"Good news John, so it looks like two were at it."

"It appears so Sir, but we still don't have a killer for Helen Spirios and DI Scooper, Sir."

"All in good time John. This is a massive result today, take the team for a drink."

"Will do, Sir."

Gammon waited until 6.00pm when DI Smarty rang.

"Sir, it's not good, we have found a body which has been sewn together. We found nothing at his house, but a neighbour said Glew had some old buildings in the middle of nowhere just outside Puddle Dale. We found it, and the smell was horrendous. He had shot himself and there was a note in his hand.

BODY PARTS

It said, *'Gammon you were to be the head on my big toy, but you ruined it. See you in hell'.*

It sent a shiver down Gammon's spine. What the hell was it all about and would they ever know?

Gammon put some sandwiches on at The Spinning Jenny. He was still concerned they didn't know who killed Helen Spirios or Sandra. This wasn't over, and John knew it.

To be continued ....

Series Three
Book Three
in the John Gammon Detective Series

Whilst writing this book a dear friend passed away suddenly, so I would like to dedicate this book to him. Kev Hawley a good friend a great character and a legend to all.

Kev was written in my book "INTRAVENOUS" as Kevin Trawley. He would often ask if he a good guy or a bad guy? Well I can tell you now, you were a good guy to all that knew you.

God bless my friend

Colin J Galtrey

Printed in Great Britain
by Amazon